S0-BDP-323

THE GIRL FROM PLAYA BLANCA

OFELIA DUMAS LACHTMAN

PIÑATA BOOKS
HOUSTON, TEXAS
1995

This volume is made possible through grants from the National Endowment for the Arts (a federal agency) and the Andrew W. Mellon Foundation.

Piñata Books are full of surprises!

Piñata Books
A Division of Arte Público Press
University of Houston
Houston, Texas 77204-2090

Cover design and illustration by Daniel Lechón

Lachtman, Ofelia Dumas.
The girl from Playa Blanca / by Ofelia Dumas Lachtman.
p. cm.
Summary: When Elena and her little brother, Carlos, leave their Mexican seaside village to search for their immigrant father in Los Angeles, they encounter intrigue, crime, mystery, friendship, and love.
ISBN 1-55885-148-8 (clothbound). — ISBN 1-55885-149-6 (paper)
[1. Brothers and sisters—Fiction. 2. Mexicans—United States—Fiction. 3. Emigration and immigration—Fiction. 4. Mystery and detective stories.] I. Title.
PZ7.L13535G1 1995
[Fic]—dc20 95-9864
CIP
AC

The paper used in this publication meets the requirements of the American National Standard for Permanence of Paper for Printed Library Materials Z39.48-1984. ∞

For Anita
who opened doors for Elena

THE GIRL FROM PLAYA BLANCA

CHAPTER ONE

She had made it this far. Nothing could change that. María Elena Vargas straightened up in the seat behind the bus driver and stared at the distant yellow lights flashing in the after-midnight blackness. This must be it, she thought, and a little tremor of fear chilled her. This must be the immigration checkpoint I heard about on the border in Tijuana. So, if nothing goes wrong here, we'll soon be in Los Angeles and on Emerald Avenue—and I'll be talking with my father.

Her fingers tightened on a thick bundle of letters on her lap. She had been saving them since she was a child and her parents had left her with her aunt in Mexico while they worked in Los Angeles. They hadn't ignored her. Every week they sent letters. Every month they sent money. And several times a year they came to see her. After her mother died, her father kept on sending letters and money. And when she went to work for Doctor Flores, the money continued to come for her brother Carlos. But five months ago all of that had stopped.

She glanced again at the lights on the highway ahead. She had made it this far, and no matter what happened here, she would not go back to Playa Blanca. Her aunt's words still stung. "You should be married by now, Elena. In a home of your own. But no. You've chosen to be an old maid!" Old maid? At seventeen? Elena swung her hair over her shoulder and shrugged. She hadn't argued. She hadn't even been angry. But then her aunt flung the final barb. "As for your father," she had said, "it seems that he's forsaken you."

Now on the seat beside hers, seven-year-old Carlos grunted and turned. "Look, Elena," he said somberly, "this trip is getting longer and longer. Are we there yet?"

A ghost of a grin twitched Elena's lips. "No," she whispered. "Go back to sleep."

Stretching uncomfortably, Elena leaned her head back on the seat and looked up at the dingy gray ceiling. If only that man behind us would stop snoring! She stole a glance at her brother. Carlos should not be here. He is going to be nothing but trouble. In a moment she leaned over him to look out the window. The bus was slowing down.

It halted with a jolt by a low wooden building that seemed to grow out of a sloping hill. The flashing red and yellow lights were above them, stretching all the way across the highway. Behind her, the snoring man awakened and growled, "What's going on here?"

The bus driver jumped into the aisle. "Stay in your seats," he said. "Immigration. It won't take long." He paused. "Did you all understand what I said?"

There were a few yeses and a few *sís*. Elena nodded, and the bus driver reached for his cap from above the dashboard and swung out the open bus door. Yes, she understood. Thanks to her friend, Sylvia Lewis, in Playa Blanca, with whom she had practiced her English. Carlos, of course, spoke only Spanish.

He sat up again. "Now we *are* there, no?" Without waiting for an answer, he pushed across her into the aisle.

"Carlos, sit down!" She grabbed at his plaid shirt and drew him into his seat as a stocky uniformed man entered the bus.

It took only a few minutes for the officer to walk to the rear of the bus and back, but it seemed a long time to her, time for her to recall the stories told in Playa Blanca about the unrelenting meanness of these officials. Finally, she shook her head. How stupid she was being. Hadn't the officer in Tijuana looked at their papers and winked and called them "gringos?" Actually, that officer had been a bit too friendly. But she had answered his questions in a cool, businesslike way, avoiding his glances—and that had been that. She squared her shoulders as the uniformed man stopped in the aisle near her.

"You," he said, pointing at her. "Where were you born?"

"Los Angeles."

"And the boy?"

"He was born there, too. He's my brother. We're going to live with our father." If the man heard her, he showed no sign of it.

"Your papers," he said.

Elena held back her irritation at the man's rudeness and dug in her purse. The birth certificates were folded in her address book, along with her father's sealed envelope and the note Sylvia Lewis had written for her to a friend named Montalvo.

She watched the officer unfold the certificates. They would tell him only where her brother and she were born, and when. They would say nothing about that sad visit after her mother died when her father had come to Playa Blanca bringing the baby, Carlos. Before her father left Playa Blanca that time, he gave her Carlos' birth record and hers. "Guard these," he told her. He had also given her the sealed envelope. "Some old papers. Nothing of importance now, but take care of them for me." And from that day to this, she had.

The officer folded the certificates and returned them to her. "Where does your father live?" he asked more gently.

"In Los Angeles." Remembering the letters on her lap, she handed them to him and pointed to the return address.

He held up the top letter. "Is this the last one? It was mailed back in November." When she nodded, he said, "This is April. Haven't you had any word from him since?"

"No," she said, "but he will be there." Of course he will be there, she told herself.

"Well," the officer said, returning the letters, "good luck to you."

Elena smiled at Carlos and let out her breath. That was over!

Within minutes the bus was on its way again. It left the brightness of the border patrol's station and moved into darkness, its lights cutting shining strips in the hillside as it turned onto the road. She was surrounded now by a cool velvet dark and the strong rhythm of the motor.

Almost immediately, Carlos was asleep again. Elena stared at the envelopes in her hands. Then she leaned her head back, closed her eyes and sighed. Of course he will be there.

CHAPTER TWO

Elena slept on and off during the last part of their journey. When she was awakened by passengers pushing through the aisle, she was surprised to see that they were stopped and in a large dark garage with empty buses lined up around them.

"Come, Carlos," she said.

After they got their suitcase, they followed the other passengers into a brightly lit waiting room. Inside, she hurried to a booth marked Information.

"Emerald Avenue. Can you tell me how to get there, please?" she asked the woman behind the counter.

The woman stooped over and dragged out a thick book which she laid on the counter between them. She fumbled through the pages. "Emerald... yeah, here it is. It's out in Venice." She directed Elena to an intersection nearby where they should wait for a bus that would take them there.

Nearby. Elena shook her head as they walked ten long blocks through the gray dawn, Carlos open-mouthed as he stared at the height of the buildings that lined the streets. He pushed close to her as they walked by doorways where homeless men slept wrapped in newspapers and rags.

"Are they beggars?" he asked. "Will they hurt us?"

"No, no," Elena said with a reassurance she did not feel. "I think they are just poor people, people with no place to go."

They found the right intersection and stood by a lamppost to wait. It was almost daylight when the bus appeared in the distance. Carlos and Elena leaned over the curbing, waving eagerly until it came to a stop beside them. They shoved the suitcase in ahead of them and took the two seats behind the driver. Elena sat stiffly on the front half of the seat, wondering how soon they would get there. But the tall buildings and wide streets seemed to go on forever. Finally, the driver looked over his shoulder and said, "This is it."

They were stopped at a corner by a gasoline station. The driver pointed away from the open bus door. "Emerald's that way," he said. "About four blocks."

Carlos helped Elena with the suitcase and they waited at the corner for the signal to change. Across the street there was a row of small shops. The bright orange door of a restaurant called La Fonda caught Elena's eye and she felt a surge of gladness. Her father had written that he sometimes ate in a restaurant named La Fonda. That meant that they were almost there.

Ten minutes later she stopped on the sidewalk in front of a house with sagging porch steps. It might once have been blue, but it was more the color of old laundry now, grayish white. The numbers 1123 hung crookedly on a pillar. A wooden rocker with a tattered magazine was on the porch by a window. But where were all the plants her father said Señora Gómez kept on the porch? She looked up and down the block. This was the right address and it was the only two-story house. It had to be the right place. She walked to the door and knocked.

When no one answered, she knocked again. In a moment she heard voices and footsteps and then the creaking of wooden stairs. The door opened, but only a few inches.

A woman's face framed by dry yellow hair looked out at her. "What the devil d'ya want?" the woman grunted. "It's not even six o'clock."

"I'm sorry," Elena said. "I know it is early, but..."

"Well, go away and come back later."

"We can't. No, please don't close the door! We're looking for Miguel Vargas. He lives here."

The woman's eyes narrowed. She peered intently at Elena and then seemed to discover Carlos and the suitcase. "Think again," she said. "My old man and me, we've lived here for more'n four months."

Elena caught her breath. Four months. And her father hadn't written for five. "He lived here with the Gómez family," she insisted. "Where did they go?"

"How would I know? You've come to the wrong place!" The woman stepped back and closed the door firmly.

"Lady, please...please," Elena called, but the only answer she got was the sound of the bolt as it slipped into place.

She turned away, then stopped and looked back. Somebody here should know *something*! But what could the walls with their peeling paint, the windows with their ragged shades, or the bolted door tell her? Nothing. Nothing at all.

She sat on the top step and dropped her head onto her knees. In all the gray morning world, there was no sound but the whirr of cars on the distant boulevard and the drip, drip of moisture falling on the sidewalk from a nearby tree. A car drove down the street and muffled music from its radio reached her. The sound was like sighing, she thought, distant, sad. How alone it made her feel.

I should have stayed in Playa Blanca. Maybe I should have gone on working for Doctor Flores, even if he didn't always keep his hands to himself. Of course, the pay wasn't enough to support Carlos and me. Still I might have managed something. Or I could have married Alfonso. If I had, I would have a home of my own now. But I would also have five ready-made children.

Elena turned and once more looked wistfully at the closed door. When she was a little girl, her father often said, "Whenever you're scared, Elenita, look over your shoulder and I will be there." And she had known what he meant. That even though he was far away, she could count on him. But where was he today? All along she had been afraid that he might not be here, but she had forced that fear into a distant corner of her mind. She had told herself that there would be no problems. She had looked only on the good side. And now? Well, she thought, there's no one to blame. It was my idea to come here.

"Come on, Carlos," she called, gathering up her things. "Come on, and don't ask where we're going because I don't know!"

There was no answer.

She took a few more steps. "Hurry up, "she said, turning. But her brother wasn't there. "Carlos! Carlos, stop hiding!" She was tired and hungry, and she could stand nothing more. "Come here right now!"

Dropping the suitcase, she ran to the side of the house. Two or three dusty shrubs and some scrawny geraniums were growing there, but there was no sign of Carlos. Then she heard his voice.

"Papá," he was calling, "Papá, where are you?"

At once she felt relieved and then puzzled. Where was he? A creaking, rustling sound came from a jacaranda tree at the rear of the house and Carlos called in a stage whisper, "Here, Elena, up here."

Above her a window was raised with a slam and the yellow-haired woman pushed her head out and shouted, "Get outta that tree, you pint-size peepin' Tom!"

Elena yelled, "Carlos, get down! Right now!"

With a splitting sound, a limb of the jacaranda arched toward the ground. Carlos hung draped on his stomach over the branch, his feet thrashing wildly. For an instant she froze, then she raced to him and grabbed his legs. "I have you. Let go!"

"That does it!" the woman at the window yelled. "I'm comin' down after you!"

Elena steadied Carlos on the ground. "Are you all right?" When he nodded, she said. "See what you did? You broke the branch. Come on, run!"

She lifted the suitcase and, carrying it pressed against her, dashed down the street with her purse dangling on her arm and Carlos at her heels. They turned the corner and kept running. They crossed one street and then another. They kept on running until Elena knew she could not take another step and they stopped. She sat on the suitcase, trying to catch her breath.

Carlos dropped to the ground. "Where's Papá?" he panted. "You said you knew, but you don't. I don't think you know anything!"

"Stop that! You got us into this trouble. And now what are you doing? Making things worse!"

He looked at her for a moment, his black eyes seeming to darken. Tears filled them and spilled over. "I am very hungry, Elena," he said.

"So am I, but the food is gone, remember? Let me think for a minute." She looked around her at the unfamiliar houses on the unfamiliar street and fought back her own tears. She didn't know where she was; she didn't know where her father was; and she didn't know what she was going to do. Carlos was right. She didn't know anything.

No, that wasn't true. There *was* one thing she knew. She knew that this was the most disappointing morning of her life—and what was even worse, she knew, too, that it wasn't over yet.

As if to prove her right, a black and white car drew to a stop at the curb beside her. She groaned. The police! That ugly, yellow-haired woman must have called them! But how could they have gotten here so fast?

A tall man in uniform got out of the passenger side of the black and white car, slamming the door. He looked at his watch. "Say, young lady, what are you doing out here so early?"

She felt her face color. In Playa Blanca no respectable woman would be found sitting idly on the streets at such an hour. She swallowed and started to answer something when from inside the police car another man's voice said, "Looks to me, Sims, like they're lost."

"They?"

"Sure. There's a kid behind that tree."

"Carlos!" Elena called, and Carlos, his eyes on his feet, walked over to her.

"So what's up?" the officer called Sims said. "Are you lost?"

Elena shook her head. "No...not lost, not really."

"What's with the suitcase? What've you got in it?"

"My clothes and his," she said quickly, annoyed at the shakiness of her voice. She raised her chin. She would *not* be afraid. "My name is María Elena Vargas, señor, and this is my brother Carlos." She gave Carlos a little push and he stepped forward and extended his hand to Sims.

"Carlos Lorenzo Vargas," he said, "*su servidor*."

Sims nodded somberly and shook Carlos' hand. "Well, Miss Vargas, tell me, where do you two live?"

Again, Elena brought out the letters and the birth certificates. She ended up telling him the whole story, even the part about the woman on Emerald Avenue. "But he did *not* break the branch, señor, not all the way. He only climbed the tree."

"Oh, I believe you," Sims said with a smile. Then, more seriously, "That's rough, your father's not being there. Could be he's following the crops. Up north, maybe."

"Picking the harvest?" she asked. "No, I don't think so. My father is a carpenter, a very good one. There must be another reason why he is not here."

"Well, until he shows up, do you have a place to stay?"

When she said no, he asked, "Any money?"

What did he mean, money? *Mordida?* Like the Playa Blanca police always expected? Were there bribes here, too? "Yes, I have money." She dug in her purse and held out her hand. "Eight dollars and fifty-two cents. Is that enough?"

"For a couple of hamburgers," Sims said, frowning. "But, anyway, it's something. Put it away." He swung around. "Bellini, come here. We have a problem."

Slowly, she put the money back. He had not taken it. Perhaps it was not enough. Well, she would wonder about that later. Right now she had to wonder what he meant by "problem."

The officer named Bellini, a stocky, curly-haired man, got out of the car and Sims and he talked briefly. Bellini turned toward them and nodded, frowning.

What would they do? Elena wondered. Take them to jail? Of course, that's what would happen. She knew that her thoughts were getting the better of her, but even so she shuddered. And at the end of the shudder came a sigh. She would have to use the letter Sylvia had given her.

"If anything goes wrong and you need help," Sylvia had told her, "don't hesitate to call on my friends, the Montalvos." And she had answered blithely that nothing would go wrong. Now, she pulled the letter from her purse and handed it to Officer Sims.

He looked at the envelope, then gave it to his partner. "Gray Ridge Drive," Bellini said. "Not a bad address, not bad at all." He fumbled for a pair of glasses in his shirt pocket and with Sims looking over his shoulder, opened the envelope and read the letter. She knew exactly what it said:

"Dear Ana and Salvador: This note is to introduce María Elena Vargas. I have known Elena since she was nine. For the past ten years I have tutored her, and in that time we have become close friends. In a remote little village like Playa Blanca, a village that looks suspiciously on "gringas" who do nothing but paint and refuse to go to church, friends are not easy to come by, so Elena's companionship has been very precious to me. (Precious also is the memory of that long-ago summer when you, Ana, and David spent two weeks with me in Playa Blanca.)

"Elena is resourceful and self-reliant, so if this letter reaches you it will be because she is truly in need of help. Please do whatever you can for her, and I will be grateful to you. Affectionately, Sylvia."

There was a rustling of paper as Bellini returned the letter to its envelope. Sims rubbed his chin. "Doctor Salvador Reyes Montalvo. Seems to me I know that name. A geologist, isn't he? Teaches at Eastmount? No? Well, anyway, I've read something about him somewhere."

Bellini said, "Maybe you have," and they walked a few steps away, where they talked again in lowered tones.

"Elena," Carlos whined, "Elena, I am hungry."

Carlos. For the moment she had forgotten him. When Sylvia had written that letter for her, they hadn't known that Carlos would follow her across Playa Blanca to the bus stop, begging to go with her. There was no mention of Carlos in Sylvia's letter. Would the Montalvos welcome him, too?

CHAPTER THREE

The officer called Sims said, "We'll make a phone call to the Montalvos and then drive you to the bus line."

"No, don't do that," Elena said hurriedly. "I'll call them myself later, but right now Carlos and I need to eat. I saw a restaurant that's not too far away."

"Where?" Sims asked.

"Over there," she said, looking around and pointing vaguely, "on that boulevard." Annoyed at herself, she added, "It doesn't matter. I can find my way there. It's called La Fonda. My father wrote that he sometimes eats there."

"So do we," said Sims with a smile.

Bellini, standing by the car, said, "I could sure use a cup of Carmen's coffee, and things are pretty dead; they're just running numbers."

Sims picked up Elena's suitcase and pushed it onto the back seat of the car. "Get in," he said. "We'll take you there."

Elena started to refuse, but at that moment a door slammed in a house across the street and an old man limped to the steps and stared at them. Almost immediately, faces appeared at the windows of other houses. Elena took Carlos' hand and they slid into the police car.

They rode only a few blocks, made a turn, and parked on the street right in front of the restaurant called La Fonda. A sign at the window said "Closed," but the officers seemed not to notice. They got out of the car and signaled them to do the same.

While she pulled the suitcase to the sidewalk, Bellini knocked at the restaurant door. At first the orange door opened only a crack, and then a woman's voice said, "Señores! Come in, come in," and it opened wide.

Bellini went inside, but Sims paused, holding the door open for Elena and Carlos. "We've brought you two hungry customers," he said to a small, plump woman near the entry, and she smiled. To Elena he said, "Wait here. We'll be right back." Then he followed Bellini and the woman through swinging doors at the back of the room into what appeared to be a kitchen.

Elena looked around. They were in a long, narrow room lined by wooden booths. The walls above the booths were decorated with posters of bullfights and costumed dancers, and there was a vase of ruffled crepe paper flowers by the cash register near where they stood. Warm, spicy smells filled the air, and the sound of voices came from behind the swinging doors.

Carlos, who had huddled in a corner of the police car, pale-faced and silent, nudged Elena. "This is funny," he whispered seriously. "This isn't a jail. It's a restaurant."

She smiled at him. "I was scared, too, Carlos. But we're not going to jail. We're going to have breakfast. The policeman said we have to wait though."

In a moment, one of the doors at the back swung open and the officer called Bellini appeared, followed by the woman.

Her black hair was pulled into a neat bun at the back of her neck, and she smoothed it away from her face as she smiled at them. "So you're hungry," she said in Spanish. She patted Carlos' shoulder and herded them into a booth. "I'm Carmen Otero, and if you two are from the state of Sonora, you have come to the right place to eat."

"We are, señora," Elena said. "And, oh, how good it all smells." Carmen Otero nodded and started to turn, but Elena touched her arm. "What we came for, señora, is to ask about my father. Miguel Vargas. Do you know him?"

The woman shrugged and rolled her eyes to the ceiling. "With all the people who come in here... *¿quién sabe?* Who knows whether I do or not? But ask my husband. He may, he may." She bustled away, stopping for an instant to throw a glance over her shoulder before pushing through the swinging door.

Carlos was grinning. "She talks Spanish, Elena, she talks Spanish, too!"

"A lot of people talk Spanish, Carlos, but don't count on it. You're going to have to learn English."

Sims came out of the kitchen and stopped at their table. “Look,” he said, “I’ve talked to Juan and Carmen, and, after you’re through eating, they’ll see that you get to your friends’ house. All right?”

Elena shook her head. “I don’t want to bother them. I can get there alone.”

“Maybe, maybe not. Let them help. They want to.”

Bellini pushed his head through the outside door. “Grab a doughnut, Sims, we’ve got a call!”

Sims waved as he hurried out the door, and Elena slumped down in the seat. “Wheeew!” she said, grinning at Carlos. The officers had been kind, but even so they had made her nervous.

When Carmen returned with a basket of hot, buttered tortillas and two steaming plates, Elena sat up. Carlos and she plunged into the welcome food. Stuffing it in like pigs, she thought and smiled happily. The eggs scrambled with *chorizo* and the refried beans were just like at home. And with that thought, she stole a glance at her brother. Was he beginning to get homesick, too?

When she finished eating, she felt warm and full and ready for almost anything. First of all, though, she had some thinking to do. After she paid for breakfast, how much money would be left? Would there be enough to get them to Gray Ridge Drive? If there wasn’t, she would ask Señora Otero if they could leave the suitcase here, and Carlos and she would walk. Why not? Gray Ridge Drive might be close by. And if it wasn’t, they would walk anyway. Holding on to that thought, she leaned back and closed her eyes—and fell asleep.

Some time later, it could only have been minutes, she opened her eyes to find Carmen Otero and a girl standing by the table. "This is my daughter Luisa," the woman said. She gave the girl a light shove and returned to the kitchen.

The girl said nothing, but gave Elena a long, appraising stare.

Elena stared back. The girl was small, with a thin neck holding up a narrow head. Her dark hair was cut too short, and straight wisps hung over her ears. Her black eyes were beautiful, Elena thought, but too large for such a small face. And, although she appeared to be about sixteen or seventeen, there was a hard look in her eyes that belonged in someone older. In Spanish Elena said that she was glad to meet her.

Luisa pushed her hands into the rear pockets of skin-tight jeans. "My mom says you can talk English, so forget the Spanish, okay?"

"Yes...okay," Elena said, puzzled.

"Not that I can't talk Spanish," Luisa said. "I just don't want to."

"Okay," Elena repeated, and then deliberately in Spanish asked Carlos, "Are you through eating?"

Carlos nodded and stuffed a wedge of tortilla into his mouth. Elena said, "Come on, then. We'll pay what we owe and leave."

"No sweat," Luisa said. "I'm not ready yet."

Elena had started to get up, but she sat down again. "What do you mean?"

Luisa jerked her chin toward the street door. "The cops told my folks your story, and now they're all tears about how sad it is that you can't find your old man." She pushed on to the seat by Carlos. "But guess who gets stuck with you? I do."

"Luisa!"

The voice was directly behind Elena, and she looked around, startled. A large, round-faced man stood by the booth. His eyes were like Luisa's, but they suited his full face better. He pushed a long, white apron aside and dug into his pants pocket, bringing out a set of keys which he placed on the table.

"Luisa," he said, "apologize to our guests for your rudeness."

Luisa's face reddened. "*Sí, Papá*," she said in a small voice. To Elena she muttered, "I'm sorry."

"Good," the man said and turned to Elena. "I am Juan Otero. You have something to ask me?"

"I am María Elena Vargas, señor, and I'm looking for my father. His name is Miguel Vargas and he lives on a street called Emerald. Do you know him? Have you seen him?"

"*Bueno!*" Juan Otero exclaimed. "I should have guessed it. You look like him. Yes, yes, I know your father."

At last! Elena nodded eagerly, surprised at how lovely the colors in the room had suddenly become. What a warm, happy place this was. She leaned across the table and squeezed her brother's arm. "Carlos, he knows Papá!"

Juan Otero said, "But you ask if I have seen him, señorita, and the truth is that I have not. Not for some time. Months, it must be."

Elena's shoulders sagged and the smile faded from her face. "How many months, señor? Four? Five?"

"About that."

"Did he talk to you? Did he say where he might be going?"

"No," he said, clearing his throat. "No, he said nothing of that."

"Are you sure? Please try to remember. I have to find him."

Juan Otero sighed, and his eyes were dark and sympathetic. "I wish I could help you, but, in all truth, I can't."

"You are sure?" she asked again, and when he answered yes, she bit her lip and fought away tears. She turned to Luisa. "Did *you* know my father?" she asked.

"No," Luisa said. "I don't pay any attention to the customers. I just give them their food."

Elena nodded. "We liked the breakfast, Señor Otero. What do we owe you?"

"Not one cent. After all, our good friends, the officers, brought you to us." He moved the keys he had laid on the table toward Luisa. "My daughter will consider it a privilege to drive you to where you are going. Is that not so, Luisa?"

"*Sí, Papá*," Luisa mumbled.

Carlos wriggled in his seat. "Elena can drive, too," he said. "Only we don't have a car."

Elena stood up. "No, we don't have a car, Carlos, but we have strong legs and good feet." To Juan Otero she said, "You are very kind, señor, but Luisa doesn't have to drive us. It will be better if we go there alone."

"Ah, now I am caught in a box," Juan Otero said. "I promised the officers that we would see you there. If not, I was to call them, and, señorita, I do not want to do that."

I do not want you to do that either, Elena thought, and gave up.

The clock on the dashboard of the Otero's blue Mustang said seven forty-five as Luisa curved the car off a boulevard called Lincoln, down a wire-fenced incline and into a short tunnel that framed a view of sandy beaches. A hazy mist was lifting. Below it, the water was a clear blue.

"It is so pretty, so peaceful," Elena said. "Almost as pretty as the ocean in Playa Blanca."

Luisa gave her a sidelong glance. She had spoken very little since they left the restaurant. Elena was grateful for that, not only because her eyes were busy with new sights and her mind with troubled thoughts, but because she did not want to hear Luisa's sour comments. They drove to a traffic light and turned inland up a steep and curving hill before Luisa spoke again.

"My father," she said, "would do anything for that cop Sims. Like making me drive you here."

Elena guessed that she was being told how unimportant she was in this early-morning chore of Luisa's and she looked straight ahead. She would not give her the satisfaction of showing any interest. Luisa, however, was determined to talk.

"It was my kid brother. That cop had something to do with his getting clean, and my father falls all over himself to thank him."

"Clean?" Elena asked, in spite of her attempt to show no interest. "What do you mean?"

"Clean means clean. Like my brother's off drugs. Cops," Luisa muttered, "are gross. And *Las Brujas* sure don't like it when my folks are so cozy with them. My mom and dad don't seem to have good sense. Look, there's you. What'd they want to get mixed up with you for? I'm trying to figure it out. What's in it for them?"

Elena thought that with those sharp words Luisa would be through, but she was wrong. "*Las Brujas*," Luisa said with a quick look at her, "are my gang. The Witches. Classy name, huh?"

Elena said nothing.

Carlos said, "*Las Brujas*. What about witches? Why don't you two talk in Spanish?"

"It has nothing to do with you," Luisa said coldly, and pressed down on the accelerator.

The car squealed around a corner and started up a hill. They left shops and hotels and tree-sheltered houses behind and began to climb through a canyon of gray-green eucalyptus trees. To her right, through high shrubs, Elena could see the gleam of the ocean now and again. Occasionally, there were gates marked "Private" and one or two narrow roads that intersected the steep, curving highway. Luisa turned the car into one of these. "Gray Ridge Drive," she said.

The trees crowded high and thick on each side of the well-kept road, shutting out the sun. Elena shivered. It was as if a gray cloud had filled the sky. Then there was a bend in the road and ahead of the trees, like a spotlight on a darkened stage, lay a miniature meadow covered with mustard in full bloom. She caught her breath. In the bright morning sun the field shimmered like a golden carpet.

The road led directly across the little meadow to a high iron fence. Behind the fence rose a three-story house made of gray stone. Its boxlike front was broken by a balcony that ran the full length of the second floor. Sunlight glinted from squares of glass in the French windows behind the balcony. This is a mansion, Elena thought, expecting Luisa to drive past the house, but Luisa curved the car through the open gate. She drove onto a gravel road that made a broad sweep in front of wide stone steps and stopped before a great wooden door.

Elena opened the car door and slowly swung her feet to the ground. She sat motionless, looking at the house. She had never been so close to anything like this before. Certainly, there was nothing like it in Playa Blanca. It was like a castle. Did people who lived in castles take in strangers?

"Are you sure this is the right place?" she asked Luisa.

"You kidding? Sure I'm sure." Luisa got out and walked around to the back of the car. She pulled their suitcase out of the trunk and dropped it on the ground. "There. You're on your own now."

"Thank you," Elena said, and helped Carlos squeeze out of the back seat.

Luisa said nothing as she started the motor. With a rough crunching of tires on gravel, she swept the car around the curve and through the gate.

Elena stared after her. What an unpredictable, rude person that Luisa was! She was not sorry to be rid of her. Turning, she found Carlos trying to pull their suitcase up the stone steps in front of the door. "Wait, Carlos," she said in a whisper. "I need a minute."

He sat on the suitcase as she drew a mirror from her purse. "Ugh," he said. "Lipstick again."

Elena ignored him as she quickly smoothed on the lip color and ran a comb through her hair. The mirror was still in her hand when she heard a soft, stirring sound above her and looked up. Waving at her from over the railing of the balcony was a dark, curly-headed little boy.

CHAPTER FOUR

Elena looked down at Carlos and then once again up to the balcony. The boy was gone.

It was clear that Carlos hadn't seen him, since he was staring intently into a stand of trees at the side of the house. "Elena," he whispered, "there! A squirrel!"

She looked where he pointed and caught a quick glimpse of a furry tail vanishing into leaf-filled branches.

Carlos looked up at her. "I should like a squirrel for a pet," he said. "They can be tamed, Elena. Is that not so?"

"I don't know. We'll ask Papá... later." She frowned and shook off a heavy sense of dejection. She didn't want to wonder what "later" might mean.

Carlos and she went up the steps to the oak door, but before they had knocked, one side of the double doors opened.

"Hi," said the boy from the balcony. "Are you looking for me?"

He was dark-haired like her brother, about the same size, and wore blue and white striped pajamas.

Carlos stared at the him. "Who is he?" he asked.

The boy took a step toward Carlos and said, "What're you doing here? What d'ya want?"

Carlos shook his head. "*No comprendo.* Listen you, can't you talk Spanish?"

Now Elena heard another voice.

"Mario, you're not dressed. Come back here!" The call was a woman's, and it came from the shadows of the entry hall.

Through the open door Elena saw that the floor of the hall was a checkerboard of russet and gray marble from which a curved staircase rose. A slim woman stood on the stairs by the balustrade, silhouetted by brilliant spears of sunlight that plunged through a window at the level of the second floor.

"Mario," the woman said, "what are you doing at the door?" Instead of answering, the boy turned and ran up the stairs past her. She gave him a backward glance and then slowly descended the stairs, the hem of her full white robe flowing gracefully from step to step. She paused at the bottom and peered toward the door. "Who's there?" she asked.

"María Elena Vargas. I have a letter for Señor and Señora Montalvo."

"Ah, yes," the woman said, moving closer to the open door. "You're one of the applicants." She frowned into the light, an oval-faced woman with velvety golden skin and black hair pulled tightly away from her forehead. Her eyes, the same startling green as the boy's, were puckered against the light and had a confused, opaque look about them.

The lady of the castle, Elena thought. All she needs is a pointed cap with a lovely sheer veil floating from its tip. The woman was only a step or two away from her now and Elena said, "Applicant? I think I should explain. I came because..."

"You're very early," the woman in white interrupted, apparently distressed. "My husband is not ready to see you. But come in, come in." She stepped aside as they entered and motioned to a tapestry-lined bench against the wall opposite the staircase. "You can sit there."

Elena said, "If you are Señora Montalvo, the letter I have is for you, too."

The woman nodded. "Of course it is. But that's all right. My husband will take care of you." She took a few steps toward the back of the hall and then paused and called over her shoulder, "I will talk to you later, of course." She turned to her left and disappeared into an archway under the staircase.

Elena closed the outside door softly. She directed Carlos to the bench.

"Listen, Elena," he said as they sat down, "how is it that they live here? This is a museum or a palace of government, no?"

"No, it's a house," she said. "I guess the Montalvos have a lot of money. Now you'd better be quiet."

Long minutes dragged by, but for a while Elena was content to rest, knowing there was nothing to do but wait. In any case, this was a lovely place to wait. The rear wall of the hall had a sliding glass door through which she could see a fenced stone terrace and, below it, a swimming pool. Beyond a high hedge of pink and white oleanders that edged the pool and the thick woods behind it was the gleaming blue of the Pacific Ocean.

Then her mood changed. Yes, she thought, this is a pretty place, a magnificent place, but I do not want to be here. I am tired, tired of traveling on bumpy buses, tired of not getting enough sleep, of worrying about Carlos, but, most of all, I'm tired of hopping from place to place like a fidgety bird. If only her father had been where he belonged...if only he had written... She straightened up on the bench. *¡Basta!* Enough, enough. She had no time for regrets. She had to think of where she was this minute and what she was going to do about it.

She had been taken for some kind of an applicant. Well, that wasn't her fault. The woman had acted strangely and quickly, not giving her time to think sensibly or to make sensible explanations. "One of the applicants," that is what the woman had said. How could she have made that mistake? Hadn't she seen Carlos? Who would show up to apply for a job with a seven-year-old along?

She looked up to the landing at the head of the stairs and the gallery that ran the width of the entry hall at the second-floor level. The arched doorways at either end, she guessed, probably led to stairways and the third floor. This house was not only elegant, it was very large, which meant that there would be many servants, not merely a cook. Everyone in Playa Blanca had a cook, no matter how little money there was. This house would have more than a cook; there would be maids, too. Maybe the Montalvos were looking for a maid.

Elena moved closer to Carlos and patted his knee. His head tilted in surprise, and she laughed. Through her laughter she heard a man's voice.

"Young lady, what are you doing here so early?" The man speaking was at the rear of the hall. He walked toward them, a frown growing on his face. "Well?"

She rose quickly. Even then it was a few moments before she spoke. The man commanded her attention. He was of medium height, stocky, with a large head and face that seemed carved of stone, so sharp was the bone structure. His gaze was fixed on her face, waiting. "Are you...are you Señor Montalvo?" she asked.

"I am Doctor Montalvo."

"Well, then, I have a letter for you," she said, and bent to her purse.

"That can wait," he said. "Do you have an appointment?"

"No, señor, I do not, but I am not one of..."

"No appointment," he said, his eyebrows rising. "You are an impulsive young woman." He glanced at his watch. "Well, you are here. I will give you five minutes, but five minutes only." He motioned her to follow him. "Leave the boy there," he said. With a lingering look at Carlos, he walked toward the rear and opened a door in the right wall.

Embarrassment, curiosity, relief...whatever feelings fought within her as she walked into the room were resolved into one: surprise. The room in which she stood was as Mexican as Playa Blanca. Its walls were adobe and the floor, brick, inlaid with tiles. There were books in heavy oak cases and a table with massive legs. A fire was burning in a raised, corner fireplace.

Doctor Montalvo held out a ladder-back chair by the table. "Sit here," he said.

She sat quickly on the rush seat, placing her purse at her feet.

He walked to the opposite side of the table, where he sat facing her. Although he had spoken in English in the hall, he now addressed her in Spanish. "Since you are here in response to our advertisement, I assume you are aware of our requirements."

"Señor," she began, but he held up his hand for silence and she saw an impatient flash in his eyes.

"To continue. You should know, then, that it is necessary for you to speak Spanish and English, both fluently, and for you to have a valid driver's license. Also, that we expect you to be moderately well-read. Some familiarity with the classics will, of course, be an additional..."

"Please!" She jumped up. "I didn't come here because of an advertisement, although I can certainly work. And I've done a lot of reading." The thought of Sylvia's bookshelves flashed through her mind. "As for a driver's license, I don't know whether mine is valid or not. But none of this matters, because I'm not here for that...even though...even though I'll soon have to find a job."

His expression didn't change as he rose from his chair. "In any case, you are obviously not qualified." Then a quizzical look came upon his face. "Tell me, young woman, why *are* you here?"

"I tried to tell you. I have a letter." She spun toward her purse and the toe of her shoe knocked it over, its contents shooting out across the floor.

With a look of complete disapproval, Doctor Montalvo bent over to pick up the papers that had landed by his feet.

Quickly, she dropped to her knees, scooping up her diary and comb and thinking, clumsy, how could you be so clumsy? She knew that her face was red and she hesitated to look up at Doctor Montalvo, but when she did, she found that he wasn't looking at her. He was staring intently at one of the envelopes in his hand.

As she rose, he said, "Your name. You didn't tell me your name."

"I'm María Elena Vargas."

He handed the papers back to her. To her surprise, he smiled, and the smile lit up his chiseled face. He was remarkably handsome. She had not noticed that before. "Well, sit down, sit down," he said.

She was glad for the support of the chair. There was no good reason for it, but she was nervous. Not merely embarrassed. No, it was something more than that...

He walked to a carved oak chest near the fireplace and poured amber liquid from a glass decanter into two stemmed glasses. "Have a drop of sherry," he said, placing the wineglass before her. "You seem to be upset."

She was. More than upset. Turned upside down, like Alice in Wonderland—and it was his fault. He had been so cold, so disapproving, and now he was smiling and pleasant and busy serving her sherry. Wine? For her? And at this hour?

"The letter," she said. "I will get it for you." She was still nervous as she fumbled through the papers on her lap: the picture of her mother; the envelope with the one word, "Tamaulipas," in her father's handwriting; the birth certificates. Finally, she found the note from Sylvia Lewis.

"There," she said, and slid it across the table.

He removed the sheet from its envelope, unfolded it, and his eyebrow lifted. She watched as his eyes went down the page, and then as they went to the top and down again. He raised his head. "A friend of Mrs. Lewis," he said, looking at—no, not merely looking at—studying her closely. Now he studied his hands, which were flattened on the tabletop. "Well, señorita, what can we do for you?"

She wanted to shout, find my father! But she said nothing. Before she could think of an answer, there was a soft knock on the door. It opened to admit the woman in the white robe.

"Salvador," she said hesitantly, "there's a young woman in the hall waiting to—oh, is there someone with you?"

Doctor Montalvo arose and walked to her. "Yes, my dear Ana, there is." He put his arm around her. "Let me introduce María Elena Vargas. She came here with a letter of introduction from your friend, Sylvia Lewis, in Playa Blanca."

Elena rose. This was better. At least now they knew who she was and why she was here.

Doctor Montalvo went on. "Her arriving today is so well-timed that I'm led to believe it is nothing short of providential. Because, you see, my dear, I am about to suggest to this young lady that she take on the job as your companion. Come, add your persuasion to mine."

Elena felt her eyes widen as she stared at Doctor Montalvo. What was this? Only a moment ago he had said that she was not qualified and now he thought her being here was "providential." In the name of all the saints, what was going on?

CHAPTER FIVE

Elena remained standing as Doctor Montalvo and his wife walked to the table.

"Sit here, Ana," he said, pulling up a chair close to Elena's.

Although morning light entered the study through French doors that led to a brick-walled patio, Doctor Montalvo walked about the room lighting several lamps. The added light revealed a collection of Indian artifacts in a cupboard by the door and a shelf displaying a row of small baskets.

At one end of the library table Elena saw a framed photograph of a younger Ana Montalvo and of a boy, a boy who was not Mario, wearing swim trunks. She sat down, her gaze on the picture. The woman and the boy were standing on a beach, rocks jutting into the sea in the background. The woman's scarf was wind-tossed, and the boy and she were laughing. Maybe it was the rocky beach that awakened unconscious longings, or maybe it was the happy faces. Elena did not know, but something stirred within her, and for an instant she, too, was on that beach, laughing while the boy shouted, "Think you're smart, don't you?" She could feel wet hair slapping against her back as she spun away from him and ran.

The moment passed. Elena glanced at the woman beside her. She was older now, of course, but still lovely, and there was a friendly warmth about her, just as in the photograph.

Doctor Montalvo walked to the chest by the fireplace and poured a glass of sherry. He turned and, glass in hand, looked at Elena steadily again. It was a challenging look, with a hint of amusement hidden in it, and she found herself gripping the sides of the chair as she prepared to speak.

"Companion? Did you say companion, señor? I'm not sure what you mean."

"What I mean, señorita," he said as he put the wineglass near his wife, "is that Mrs. Lewis' letter has brought me great relief. Finding the right companion for my wife was proving difficult. You speak excellent English and Spanish, and you are recommended to us by my wife's friend. Unless you have a previous obligation, I would like you to take the position."

"But Sylvia Lewis didn't recommend me as a companion—or anything else."

Ana Montalvo reached over and touched her knee. The green eyes seemed to shed a veil as she asked, "You've come from Sylvia? How is she?" She peered toward the door. "She's not here?" A smile, half-completed, disappeared as she said, "No, of course not." And then it returned, bright and warm and with a hint of self-reproach as she added, "After all, I let you in, didn't I?"

"Sylvia's fine," Elena said. "I mean, she was when I left three days ago. It's because of her that I'm here. There's a letter. I gave it to your husband."

Doctor Montalvo said, "Shall I read it to you, Ana?"

"Please."

When the letter was read, Señora Montalvo bent forward and with deliberate, almost painstaking care set her wineglass down at the edge of the table. Then she pushed it slowly toward the center. With the glass settled, she turned to Elena. "You did the right thing in coming to us. What can we do for you?"

"I...I don't know. I came here to live with my father," she said, and then told them the story of her disappointing morning. "Until I find him, I'll need to work. But what is the work of a companion, señora? I'm not sure I can do that."

"Nor am I," the woman said. "But we can give it a try. You want to work and I want to help you. So we have a beginning."

"There's one small problem, Ana," her husband said. "This young lady doesn't have a driver's license."

"Does that matter? Mr. Addison can take me where I need to go."

"Addison has other duties. Yes, the driving does matter, but perhaps we can solve that difficulty." He turned to Elena. "We'll provide driving lessons as a part of your pay. Does that seem fair?"

Elena nodded. "I can drive," she said. "But maybe not in a city. Yes, that's fair. I will need to practice city driving."

"In that case," Doctor Montalvo said, "it is agreed that you'll remain with us, at least for a while. There is a lovely room for you and also time for some of your own pursuits. But you and I can meet before dinner to discuss details. Take the morning to settle in. This afternoon Ana and you will want to get to know one another."

"Thank you," Elena said, "thank you both." She was not dreaming. All of this was really happening. It was still early morning, but so much had happened since leaving the bus in midtown Los Angeles that days might as well have passed. For the last two hours events had tumbled one on top the other, and now here she was, a part of this unbelievable conversation. The Montalvos, it seemed, had decided. She was to work in this lovely house for the elegant lady beside her. And there would even be time to search for her father. But when she remembered Carlos, her gladness disappeared. What had she been thinking about? She swallowed hard and said, "Señora Montalvo, I've made a mistake. I can't be your companion. There's my brother. I have to take care of him."

As if in response to a cue, the door of the study burst open and Carlos plunged into the room. "Elena!" he shouted.

Ana Montalvo turned. "What is this?" she said. "Mario, where are you? Why didn't you boys knock?"

"It wasn't me, Momma!" Mario called from the hall. "It was him! He's the one!"

Carlos rushed to Elena and tugged at her. "I do not like it here," he said in Spanish. "Let's go."

"What are you doing, Carlos?" she whispered angrily. "Why are you behaving this way?"

"Me? Not me. It's him! Ask him."

"I'm very sorry," Elena said. "I don't know what this is about, but I'll take..."

Doctor Montalvo held up his hand impatiently, asking for silence. "Mario, come here!"

Mario pushed his head through the door. He put one foot in and then another. Slowly, he dragged himself across the room, stopping a yard or so from his father's chair. Doctor Montalvo motioned Carlos to come toward him. Elena took her brother gently by the shoulders and urged him forward until he was standing by Mario.

"All right, young man," Doctor Montalvo said to Carlos, "tell me. What is this all about?"

"*No comprendo, señor*," Carlos muttered, his face reddening. Elena thought, why, yes, we have been talking in English since his wife came into the study. "*No comprendo, señor*," Carlos repeated.

"What happened, Carlos?" Elena said. "Doctor Montalvo wants to know."

Carlos pointed at Mario. "That clown has been making fun of me, imitating my Spanish like an ugly parrot! I am going to beat him up if he does it again! Tell him, Elena!"

Well, that did it. Elena cringed, as if a blow had been struck. Carlos had ruined any chance they had left. He tugged at her sleeve.

"Tell him, Elena!" he repeated. "You have to, because that Mario is so dumb that he can't even talk Spanish!"

Elena looked into Salvador Montalvo's face. Something came and went there. It was only the slightest hint of an expression, but it was threatening. She pulled Carlos close to her.

With a thud, Doctor Montalvo flattened his hands on the table. "He will speak it soon," he said, looking from Mario to his wife. "I intend to take care of that."

"I could teach him, *señor*," Elena said, and wondered why she had decided so eagerly to step into quicksand. There was a message shifting back and forth between Salvador Montalvo and his wife that she could see but could not understand. She stiffened. What had she done? But Doctor Montalvo, it seemed, had not heard her. He spoke to his son.

"It's time for your school bus. Go. Wait outside." He strode to the glass doors and remained there, facing the patio. Mario went to his mother and gave her a kiss on the cheek. Ana hugged him and whispered seriously in his ear.

When the door had closed behind his son, Doctor Montalvo swung around. "Yes," he said, "you could teach him Spanish." So he *had* heard. "But I think that your brother will teach him better."

"Carlos?" Elena said, unbelieving, and he gave a curt nod.

Ana's face was flushed, but she said nothing as her husband spoke to Elena. He explained that if she could control Carlos, then the position was still hers.

"Of course, I will expect Mario to learn Spanish," he said. "Which means that the boys must spend a great deal of their time together. Which also means that they must be able to get along." There was a short silence. "I will arrange for Carlos to attend Mario's school—on a temporary basis, of course. I know the headmaster; it should pose no problem. I want them to be together as much as possible." He turned to Carlos and in Spanish said, "*Bueno*, Carlos, how would you like to live here?"

"Me? Here?" Carlos' eyes widened as he looked from Doctor Montalvo to his sister. "Elena, *¿qué dice?* What is he saying? Do we really get to live here?"

"Absolutely," Doctor Montalvo said.

Elena looked curiously at the man at the window. He had decided in seconds what he must do about Carlos—actually, what he must do about his son's Spanish—and a plan to give meaning to his decision was already clear in his mind. He was an intelligent man, that was certain, and he was kind. Carlos and she were a pair of troublesome strangers, and he was going out of his way to be helpful. "I can manage Carlos, *señor*," she said, nodding firmly. "He will get along with Mario."

Later, as Carlos and she waited for the housekeeper to show them to the rooms they were to share, she wondered if she had spoken from conviction or from necessity.

CHAPTER SIX

"I'm Mrs. Addison," said the stout woman who came from the back of the entry hall to meet them at the foot of the stairs. She wiped her hands on the edge of a white apron and tucked a loose strand of waving gray hair into an old-fashioned bun at the back of her neck. "I'm Mrs. Montalvo's housekeeper. Been with her for more'n twenty years. Sara, she's the only other help, except for Mr. Addison, of course, came much later. Hired by Doctor Montalvo, don't you know."

Elena wondered if she had heard a sniff. She was sure that she had heard disapproval.

"And since she's not here today," Mrs. Addison continued, "I'll show you to your rooms myself." She paused, her hand on the railing. "You *do* talk English, don't you?"

"Yes. Yes, I do. My name's María Elena Vargas. I am called Elena. And this is my brother Carlos."

"Dear, dear, for a moment there I took him for Mario. Not that they look alike," she added hurriedly, "except, of course, for that thatch of curly hair. You boys will hit it off fine, now, won't you?"

Carlos looked up at her and grinned. Elena said, "I'm sorry. I forgot to say that my brother doesn't speak English."

"That so? Well, he'll soon pick it up," Mrs. Addison said comfortably. "Looks like a bright boy. Come along now." She started up the stairs.

The room to which Mrs. Addison led them was in the right wing of the second floor. It was a large corner room, with a balcony facing south and a bay window on the west wall. The carpet was a rich avocado green, and the sheer white curtains and bedspread on the high, cushiony bed were scattered with flowers of pale yellow and apricot. There was a small corner fireplace. On its mantel, a porcelain clock, too, was sprigged with tiny yellow and orange flowers. Elena dropped the suitcase, turned full circle, and drew in her breath.

Mrs. Addison smiled. "It's a pretty room, isn't it?" she said. "And a comfortable one. That's a good-drawing fireplace, and there's plenty of firewood downstairs in the workroom. Mr. Addison laid a fire for you, just ready for the lighting, but after this you'll be needing to help yourself."

"I will, of course, I will," Elena said. "That was very nice of him. He must have a lot to do."

"He does indeed," Mrs. Addison said, and this time there was a sniff. "There's more to do than a man can handle. It's that fiesta of Doctor Montalvo's that's putting the load on us, don't you know. But it will soon be over." She turned to a door on the wall opposite the bay window. "This leads to the bathroom, and the door on the other side connects with a small room that's a sitting room or study.

The couch there makes into a good, firm bed. That'll be the young man's. Carlos, is it?"

"Yes, Carlos," Elena said. "And where is he?"

"On the balcony. Look at him. I dare say he's checking out the trees to see which ones are meant for climbing."

"You read minds, Mrs. Addison. Because that's just what he's doing."

Mrs. Addison pulled the drapes open all the way. "Mr. David could tell him about the trees. He had them all checked out before we'd been one full day in this place, and him hardly a day over six. He was an active one, and adventurous. Not a bit like Mario."

"Mr. David?"

"Miss Ana's older son. Full grown now, of course, into a fine, strapping young man. And not one of your wild ones. Not Mr. David. Oh, he's got red blood in his veins, and he's a handsome one, but he's a good son, kind and devoted to his mother."

"Does he live here?"

"Dear me, no. He's a law student. Up to all hours researching and studying, don't you know. Wouldn't do at all for him to live at home. Besides, Doctor Montalvo and David..." She stopped suddenly, patting the drape unnecessarily to straighten its folds. "Doctor Montalvo and David," she repeated more thoughtfully, "are not at all alike. He, Doctor Montalvo, I mean, is an archie-ologist. Teaches at a university. Eastmount. But there, you wouldn't be interested in all of that, now would you?"

"Yes, I would," Elena said. "After all, I'm going to work here."

"Well, that's kind enough. But I expect you need your rest more than you do my chattering." She moved firmly to the door, but once there hesitated and turned. "It's nice to have young people about the house again. Mario needs company. He misses his brother, don't you know." With that she was gone, but Elena had the feeling that with even the slightest bit of encouragement Mrs. Addison would have stayed and talked.

Elena called Carlos, and he came in reluctantly. "There are trees out there," he said, "with branches that are of the best for climbing. This is a fine place."

She grinned and said, "There is a bathroom in there, Carlos, with a tub that is of the best for bathing. Fill it with warm water and get in. And wash well. I'll rest a bit until you're through." She kicked off her shoes and lay on top the bed, glancing at the clock on the mantle. It said twenty minutes after ten.

It was two-thirty when she awakened. She sat up, rubbed her eyes, and then lay back on the pillow. The room was a part of a beautiful dream, and she did not want to awaken. Abruptly, she sat up again. No, this was not a dream, and in a real, wide-awake life, a man called Doctor Montalvo had told her to spend the afternoon with his wife. Now the afternoon was half gone.

"Carlos," she called, and when there was no answer, she swung her feet to the floor and went through the bathroom to look for him. Carlos was not to be found, but there was evidence that he had bathed: little lakes of water dotted the floor, a large wet towel lay huddled in a corner, and soapy bath water had painted a ring around the tub.

She dressed quickly and hurried down the curved staircase to the entry hall. She wanted to find the kitchen and Mrs. Addison. Which way now? Across from where she was standing, next to the tapestry-covered bench on which she had waited earlier, was a high double door. She tiptoed to it and turned the knob. She was looking into a large elegantly furnished room with a high ceiling from which hung glass chandeliers. There was a grand piano at the far end. She closed the door quietly and glanced again around the entry hall. Opposite the door to Doctor Montalvo's study was the archway through which Ana Montalvo had disappeared earlier. Mrs. Addison, she remembered, had come from that direction, too.

She started across the hall. Before she had taken two steps, she heard the sound of a door slamming. Then that of an angry mutter. "You have no right, Montalvo! No right at all!" With his head thrust forward, a dark-haired man in jeans and sneakers charged toward her.

She moved to the right, then to the left to avoid him, but she failed. "Ah-h-h!" she gasped as he bumped into her. She clutched his shirt to keep from falling, and the strong grip of his hands on her arms steadied her. She pushed away and said, "Oh, I'm sorry!"

"Yeah? Well, so am I," he said, and strode past her and out the front door.

She smoothed her dress, tightening its belt with unsteady fingers, and glared at the closed door. She was left with an impression of thick black hair and large sunglasses, and a rage that was almost touchable. Whoever he was, he was not only angry but rude. And rude, not only to her, but to Doctor Montalvo. With one last look at the closed outside door, she headed toward the archway. She had to find Carlos and then Señora Montalvo.

The corridor under the staircase led to a room that was papered in a cheery ivy pattern. An oval table in the center held a bowl of white daisies. This was a place for eating, so the kitchen had to be nearby. When she looked through an open door on her right, she found the kitchen, Mrs. Addison, and Carlos. He gave her a swift look, flushing a slow, unflattering red. Carlos was perched on a high stool by a counter peeling potatoes.

Mrs. Addison winked at her. "I've fed him lunch and put him to work."

"Good. I'm glad. I was afraid he'd be in the woods looking for squirrels."

"Oh, he'll see my family of squirrels when he's through with the potatoes," Mrs. Addison said. "But he still has some to go."

"You made him understand? I didn't think he would."

"Did you now," Mrs. Addison said primly. "Well, I've picked up a word or two of Spanish."

Elena said, "Where can I find Señora Montalvo? I should have been with her long ago."

"She told me not to hurry you. Take time for some lunch." Elena shook her head. Mrs. Addison pushed a glass of milk across the counter. "There. Drink that. It's not enough, but I can see you're not going to stop for more." She waved her arm. "You went right by Mrs. Montalvo's sitting room. The plant room, she calls it. It's off the corridor. To your left as you walk back."

Elena gulped down the milk and found the door in the hall. At her knock Señora Montalvo called, "Come in."

She was standing by a round table, a small watering can in her hand. Elena took in the white wicker furniture, the baskets and pots of hanging plants and the view of the pool and the woods all in one glance. Her gaze returned to the woman at the table. She was dressed in white wool pants and a beige and white silk shirt. The lady of the castle in modern clothes, Elena thought as, once again, she smoothed the skirt of her dress.

Ana Montalvo put the watering can down and said, "I've been looking forward to our visit. Come sit by the window where I can see you better." She motioned to an armchair. "Now," she said when they were seated, "let us talk. I know your town of Playa Blanca. I visited Sylvia Lewis there."

Close to two hours later, when she was ready to leave, Elena realized that she had done most of the talking. The other woman had listened as she told about her reasons for leaving Playa Blanca and of Carlos' pleading to come with her. "The city is exciting," she ended, "but already I miss Playa Blanca. The distances here are so great. Playa Blanca is so small that my cousin Carmen and I can walk from one end of it to the other in ten minutes. And every face we see belongs to someone we know. Of course," she added, "those are the very reasons why everybody in Playa Blanca knows everybody else's business."

"Yes," the older woman said. "That was my impression when I visited there."

"Well, then, Señora Montalvo," Elena said, "you know that the people of my town are courteous and good, but that they do not open themselves up to strangers."

Ana Montalvo nodded and said, "Privacy is important. And Playa Blanca is a lovely place. I can see why so many Americans are hurrying to retire there. Well, I think we are through for today, Elena."

She was dismissed. Elena walked slowly to the kitchen and when she found no one there, turned and went up the curved staircase to her room. Hanging from the doorknob, she found a note from Mrs. Addison. "Carlos is with Mario in the library.

Mario's tutor is with them. Doctor Montalvo will see you at five-thirty."

Somewhere, perhaps in the salon, a clock chimed the half-hour as she knocked on the door to Doctor Montalvo's study. Once more she sat on the ladder-back chair across the table from him. Once more she listened to his precise voice, this time explaining details of her position.

Each morning at nine, he said, she was to report to his wife so that they could plan their day. She was to serve as secretary and driver, as well as companion.

"Secretary? But here is the thing, señor. I cannot type. Perhaps I am the wrong person."

"Let me be the judge of that." Had she imagined a hint of amusement in the look he threw her? "Reassure yourself, señorita. My wife's correspondence is mostly social and, therefore, done by hand. You will have no problem there. Do you like to walk?" He didn't wait for an answer. "Ana, before her sight was impaired, was a great walker. She knows all the footpaths in these woods."

Before her sight was impaired. So I was right, Elena thought. There is something wrong with Señora Montalvo's eyes.

"You're wondering about my wife's eyesight." Was it possible—no, of course, not. And yet the man seemed to have read her mind.

"I won't go into details," he said, "except to say that it is something she must learn to live with. With medication, there is no reason why she should not write and read and drive, in other words do all the things you have been hired to do, but lately her vision has worsened. We expect the setback to be temporary." He frowned and looked momentarily at the case with the Indian artifacts. Then he turned back to her and talked about the boys.

She would spend time with them in the afternoons and evenings, lending a hand with their schoolwork. Carlos, he told her, would attend Loring School starting the next day. He would be tested and placed. "Some of the testing will be oral and in Spanish. Do not worry. We do not expect too much of Carlos."

She stiffened in her chair as a little flame of anger sparked within her. Carlos was not dumb. How dare Doctor Montalvo assume such a thing!

"Each night at seven," he went on, "you and your brother will join us for supper in the dining room." He must have seen the question in her eyes because he added, "You are our guests and will be treated as such. Your second role, that of companion, is a matter of convenience to us and we appreciate it."

He shuffled through some papers and said, "Your driving lessons will begin on Saturday morning." As to your salary, it will be minimum wage to begin. You may have a week's pay in advance, if you wish."

"No, thank you. I will accept my pay only when I have earned it."

His eyebrow rose as he nodded curtly. Then he stood up. The conference was over.

Later, after Carlos was asleep and she was getting ready for bed, Elena thought again of her talk with Doctor Montalvo. He had been nothing if not generous. There was no reason for her discomfort and yet there it was inside her, unmovable, solid and heavy like a rock.

She pulled the drapes back and night lights from the swimming pool area brightened the room. That big, beautiful bed was all hers. No narrow cot in a small room shared with three cousins. She, alone, would sleep in this lovely room. The luxury of the house was hard to get used to. Eating supper in that elegant dining room had been like being in a movie. And her job! All she had done today was talk. Maybe tomorrow the real work would begin. But no matter what her duties would be, they certainly would be better than washing out dirty test tubes for Doctor Flores in Playa Blanca—and fighting off his hands.

She got into bed, pulled the soft quilt up to her chin, and sighed. She had hoped to be spending this night in a three-room apartment on the second floor of a house on Emerald Avenue. There, Carlos and she would have been sleeping on the floor, maybe, or on a couch, but it would not have mattered, so long as it was with her father. Right now, right this very minute, that is exactly where she wanted to be.

But when at last Elena fell asleep, she wasn't thinking of her father. She was thinking about the angry young man who had bumped into her in the entry hall.

CHAPTER SEVEN

Elena awakened early the next morning, but not before Carlos. When she opened her eyes, there he was, huddled in a wing-backed chair by the bay window. His face was puckered into an angry frown.

"I am not going," he grumbled when he saw that she was awake.

Elena bounced up in bed. "What are you talking about?"

"I am not going," Carlos repeated.

"Where?"

"Do not think that I am, Elena."

"Why do you drag this out, Carlos? Like throwing scraps to a chicken. What are you talking about?"

"That school. I am not going to that school. I came here to see Papá."

"You came here because I let you. And I let you because you promised to do what I told you. *Bueno*, I am telling you you have to go. And what's more, I'm telling you to be nice to Mario."

Carlos stood up. "Elena," he said, "I want Papá."

She threw off the blankets and put her feet on the floor. "So do I, but until we find him, we have other things to do. And going to that school and getting along with Mario are two of the things you will do, or somehow—I don't know how—I'll find a way to send you back to Playa Blanca! Now, go put your clean pants on."

Elena and a subdued Carlos had breakfast in the kitchen before they went out the front door to wait for the school bus. Mario, spotless in a white shirt, creased gray pants and blue monogrammed jacket, was there ahead of them.

"Eh, Mario, what goes?" Carlos called in Spanish. And then, with a flicker of a grin. "Do you even know what that means?"

Mario shrugged in a gesture of disinterest and said a sullen "Hullo." Then, pushing his hands into his pants pockets, he walked to the end of the cement steps and sat down.

Elena watched her brother move to the other end and lean on a large pot that held a scarlet azalea. She looked from one to the other and wondered if they would ever get along. And it was up to her to see that it happened. She sighed and leaned against the door. The morning was filled with sounds: the whirr of wings and chirping of birds, the scurrying of squirrels as they moved from tree to tree. She stared beyond the gate to the little meadow. The morning sun was bright and the trees threw elongated shadows across the golden field, patterning it with diagonal stripes. Even from this distance she could see winged insects busy around the mustard blooms. Within minutes, a polished blue mini-bus sped across the meadow and entered the gates.

Elena bent down to Carlos. "Please be good today," she whispered. "We need a place to live, remember."

"You already told me."

The bus had rounded the drive and was stopping with a coarse, scraping sound on the gravel by the door. Mario got up and motioned to Carlos to come. Elena gave her brother a little shove. At the bus steps, Mario let Carlos get on ahead of him, and Elena thought, he, too, has been told to be on good behavior. She had a tug of feeling for the little boy in the well-pressed pants and jacket. He will behave, she thought, because he is afraid of his father, but only the saints know how Carlos will act.

When the bus disappeared beyond the yellow field, she felt a sudden despondency. Empty. She felt as empty and idle as a sailboat without wind. She had never lived a day without the protection of her father. She had felt his strength and his constancy in his letters. She had always known that he was as close as a telephone call. And now he was... nowhere. No, no, he had to be somewhere. But instead of finding that "somewhere," here she was once again leaning on the protection of others—and feeling useless.

Elena glanced once more at the golden meadow and then went up to her room. She had unpacked their clothes the night before and the suitcase was stored in the closet. Now she had to find a safe place for her papers. She looked around the room, her gaze stopping at the clock on the mantle. Its wooden base was large and it was heavy. Tilting the clock carefully, she slid her father's envelope and the birth certificates under it. Her diary, her mother's picture, and her father's bundled letters she returned to her purse. Glancing at the clock, which reassured her that she had ten minutes to spare, she went out on the balcony.

The Montalvos' property sloped downward, giving the back of the house a level lower than that of the front. A young man wearing a worn white tee shirt, jeans and sneakers and carrying a tool box strode across the sloping lawn. Sunlight glinted from his gold hair and beard. He was tall, and his long shadow angled far ahead of him as he walked toward the house. She watched as he opened a door directly below Ana's plant room and disappeared through it. Who was he? The older son? No. The boy in the photograph had black hair. Maybe he was an employee. Still, Mrs. Addison had said that there was no other help but a woman named Sara. Elena shrugged. In any case, it didn't concern her, and it was time to start her first day of work.

In a matter of minutes she was knocking softly on the door of the plant room.

"Enter." Ana Montalvo, wearing a bulky sweater and wool pants, was standing near the hearth, staring into a fire in the white-framed fireplace.

Elena waited a bit and then asked, "Is there... is there something you want me to do?"

The woman at the fireplace looked up. "I'd like you to write some letters. You'll find notepaper in the desk drawer. The letters I'm replying to are in that basket. Read them over and we'll start."

"Aloud?"

"No. I can still manage to read most of my letters with a magnifying glass, and patience. There are even days when I can read without a magnifying glass. My eyes play games with me, you see. Sometimes I can see better than others."

Elena thought of the stemmed glass which had been placed so close to the edge of the table in the study. Yes, she had had trouble seeing in that room yesterday.

Ana Montalvo smiled as she tilted her head. "As a matter of fact, Elena, I can see you quite well today. You're a very pretty girl. I can see the print of your dress, too. White flowers on blue. You're so feminine. Perhaps it's that you wear dresses, not pants as I do."

"I would wear pants, too, but in Playa Blanca my aunt, the church, and my employer all frowned on them. So I have none."

Ana Montalvo said, "Come here, will you? I have an idea." She moved close to her, matching shoulders. "There. What do you think? Are we about the same size?"

Elena nodded.

The older woman patted her arm. "Don't be shy. Answer me."

"Yes, señora, yes, I think we are."

"Well, then, I have some things for you—if you want them."

Elena hesitated. She had never worn anyone else's clothes before. "In this family, we don't accept charity," her aunt had said proudly when Sylvia had once tried to give her a sweater. But Ana's clothes would be so special that even her aunt would approve.

"They're fairly young-looking pants and shirts," Ana was saying. "Even a couple of bikinis that have never been worn." She laughed a tight little laugh. "Salvador objects to my wearing bikinis. He is quite conservative about bathing suits." Again she patted Elena's arm. "They're nice clothes, but they're not jeans and boots, so I'll understand if you don't want them."

"Oh, I want them," she said. "Thank you very much."

Across from her, Ana Montalvo smiled and nodded as Elena sat down at the desk. "Well, fine. I'll have Sara bring them to your room this afternoon."

Elena stared at the papers on the desk. Even through her feelings of gladness, she felt dazed. Santa Teresa, she thought, why am I so lucky? Why are all these good things happening to me? This morning I awakened believing I was still in a dream. And now? Now, except for the worry of my father, I would be sure I was living in a fairy tale, with Ana my fairy godmother.

Elena stirred, trying to move away from her thoughts. She picked up the envelopes and stacked them neatly before her. "I'll read the letters now."

The first letter was from a woman's club, asking Mrs. Salvador Montalvo to serve on its board of governors. Elena read the letter slowly, wondering what a board of governors was and what Señora Montalvo's answer would be. The next was addressed to Mrs. Ernesto Martel. Ernesto Martel? The movie star? How strange. The letter was asking old friends once again to contribute to a drug-prevention program. She stared at it, wondering what it was doing here. "This letter is for Mrs. Ernesto Martel," she said as calmly as she could. "What shall I do with it?"

Ana turned away from the window and said, "We'll respond to it. It's for me. That used to be my name."

"Then he. . . he was your husband!"

"Yes, Elena, he was my husband. And you obviously know who he was."

"How could I not?" Ernesto Martel was the man whose autographed picture she had kept under her pillow. When he was killed in a sailing accident, although she was only nine, she had mourned for weeks. "Everyone knows him."

Señora Montalvo laughed. "Just about everyone, I suppose. His pictures were popular not only in the United States, but all over the world. Even in Playa Blanca, it seems." She was silent for a moment and then said, "This was Ernesto's favorite room. This and the library. He loved it there in the afternoons." She sighed. "After we finish the letters, Elena, we'll go there and pick out some books."

Five carefully written letters later, Ana Montalvo led the way to the library. It was a long narrow room directly below Elena's bedroom. The west wall of the library was covered with windows, making the eucalyptus grove outside a part of the room. One corner was for T.V. watching, a circle of comfortable chairs facing a large television set. Elena felt light-headed. She was standing in Ernesto Martel's favorite room!

Together, Ana and she selected three books for reading aloud and returned to the plant room shortly after noon.

"I'm going to have a tray sent upstairs and then have a little rest," the older woman told her. "Come back at two-thirty." She paused. "And, Elena, please call me Ana. I want you to think of me as a friend, not as an employer."

"I'll try, really I will, but I'm not sure that I can."

"I'll help you," Ana said with a smile. "Now, go on. Enjoy your lunch."

Lunch was served buffet-style in the breakfast room. That morning Mrs. Addison had told her that between twelve and one, lunch was eaten at each person's convenience. "Doctor Montalvo will eat at the college today," she had said. "Other times he's here. Alone, or with a student or two, back from one of those field trips. No warning of it, don't you know. Well, I always fix plenty, just in case."

Now Elena walked into the ivy-papered breakfast room and found it empty. The walnut sideboard held a steaming casserole, a platter of cold meat, and a wooden bowl with salad. After filling her plate, Elena pulled out a chair at one end of the table. But when she heard voices and laughter coming from the kitchen, she carried her plate in there. Mrs. Addison and a thin, balding man were seated at a small table near an east window.

"If you don't mind," Elena said, "I'd like to eat in here with you."

Mrs. Addison looked up and patted her mouth with a large cloth napkin. "I dare say it's all right," she said in a warm voice. "This is my husband Henry. Come along then, don't stand there. Sit down with us."

Elena slid into a chair that faced French doors. Henry Addison nodded and in a few minutes he was through with his lunch and gone. Mrs. Addison chatted her way through two cups of tea and then busied herself in the pantry.

Elena finished her coffee, looking out at a stretch of lawn between the two wings of the house. At the end of the opposing wing, *her* wing, there was an outside staircase that she decided must lead to the hallway by her room. When she was through with lunch, she cut across the lawn toward the staircase. Halfway there she stopped. Sounds of hammering came from below the plant room. Mrs.

Addison had said that firewood was kept in the workroom, and this must be the place. She had wondered how she would carry firewood through the house, but the outside stairs gave her the answer.

Shrubbery almost hid the windows of that lower level, growing so close to the door that she might not have found it had it not been for the stepping stones. The hammering continued as she opened it and stepped inside. A pool table was in the center of the room and folded card tables and chairs were stacked against the walls. Broken pieces of a wooden crate and crumpled newspapers were scattered on the floor by a door on the far wall.

Where would the firewood be? She looked under the pool table and then circled it, heading for the far door. Before she reached it, the door opened and the bearded blond man she had seen that morning stepped out.

"What're you doing here?"

"Looking for the firewood."

"Firewood? Here?" His eyes narrowed.

"Yes. Mrs. Addison said it would be here. In the workroom."

He shook his head. "You're in the wrong place."

"But this morning I saw you carrying a tool box in here. And where else does one carry tools but to a workroom?"

He was watching her curiously. "Well, this isn't it. Thought old Henry was in charge of firewood."

"Perhaps he is, but Mrs. Addison said I should get my own. In the workroom," she added stubbornly.

"Well, you'll just have to talk to Addie about that again," he said. Then he grinned and his blue eyes sparkled. "Don't look so put down. I don't bite, honest. Here, don't go away empty-handed." He bent over and bundled up the pieces of wood on the floor, wrapping them in the newspapers that lay beside them. "This'll burn." He stood up and grinned as he looked down at her. "You're new here, aren't you?"

She nodded.

"Figures. You working or visiting?"

"Working."

"Good. Then I'll be seeing more of you. I'm Jim Donald, an assistant of sorts to Professor Montalvo."

"I'm Elena, María Elena Vargas," she said with a smile, "a companion of sorts to Señora Montalvo. Do you live here?"

"I come and go." He gave her a wide grin. "I'm an adventurer at heart. Now you see me, now you don't."

"I see," she said, and put out her arms. "I'll take the wood now. And thank you."

He handed her the bundle and held the door open.

In her room she dropped to her knees by the hearth. The papers rustled crisply as she crumpled them and tossed them on the grate. She leaned forward to pile on the wood, but stopped as she saw that the newspapers were printed in Spanish. Pressing a couple of sheets out on the floor, she found that they were only a couple of weeks old. But what held her eyes was that they had been printed in Matamoros, in the Mexican state of Tamaulipas.

She sat back. In her mind's eye she could see a firm, familiar handwriting in black ink on a yellowing surface, the capital "T" done with a flourish. "Tamaulipas." That was what was written on the sealed envelope her father had given her for safekeeping so many years ago.

CHAPTER EIGHT

Tamaulipas. Elena scanned the papers. Although they were printed in a large town, not a village like her own Playa Blanca, bits of the news were much the same. A street was being rerouted because of earth slippage. A cow had been stolen from the Convent of the Sisters of Grace, and the thief was asked to return it with no fear of reprisal. Water from the Palo Seco well was no longer safe to drink. She shrugged. There was nothing here to interest anyone in Los Angeles, except perhaps Doctor Montalvo, who liked to surround himself with Mexican things, and who wanted his son to speak Spanish fluently. He probably received all kinds of Spanish-language papers.

Elena crumpled up the papers again and returned them to the grate. She finished laying the fire and was brushing off the hearth when she heard a knock on the door.

"Come in, please."

The door opened, admitting a small dark woman carrying a plastic garment bag across her arms. "Señora Montalvo sent this," she said, her eyes shifting away from Elena's face.

"You brought the clothes!" Elena held out her arms and took the bundle. "Thank you. Are you Sara?"

The small woman's eyes shifted again, circling the room. "Yes. And you are María Elena, no?"

"Elena, please. Just Elena."

"As you wish. There is also a young man? Your little brother?"

"Yes. Carlos is at school with Mario."

"What a thing," Sara said dryly. "A private school. You are being treated well, aren't you?"

Elena gave Sara a sidelong glance and decided at that instant that she would have great trouble in ever liking this woman. "We have good fortune, Carlos and I," she said.

Sara edged toward the closet. "Do you want me to help you put the clothes away?"

"No, thank you."

"Are you sure? They are very pretty clothes, and I will hang them with great care."

"Thank you, Sara, but I want to look at them first."

"Then I'll get back to my work." She went into the hall and closed the door behind her.

Almost immediately, Elena forgot Sara as she unzipped the plastic bag and brought out the garments one by one. And one by one she admired them. They were just what she would have picked out for herself—if she had won the National Lottery. She tried them all on. They were perfect. An hour later, when she returned to the plant room, she was wearing blue-denim pants and a cotton knit shirt.

Elena was eager to tell Señora Montalvo how happy she was with the clothes and how lucky it was that almost all of them fit well. But Ana seemed distant, so all she said was, "I love the clothes. Thank you."

Ana said, "I hoped you would," and immediately handed her a book. It was a collection of short stories.

"Read the Hemingway first," she said, "and then Steinbeck. Later, we'll hear some Lawrence." But after the first story she said, "You read very well, Elena, but that's enough for today." She looked out the window for a few moments and then turned and said, "Let's go for a walk in the woods. I miss my walks."

Elena gave her a questioning look, then quickly asked, "When do you want to go? Now?" A walk? Through dark woods? There would be rocks on the path and fallen limbs, and what would she do if Ana fell and hurt herself?

"Yes. Don't worry, I know the trails well. I'll point them out to you. And, Elena," she added gently, "we'll be extremely careful."

The path into the woods began twenty yards or so behind the hedge of oleanders at the boundary of the Montalvos' property. Although Ana had walked from the main house without help, she stretched out her hand to Elena at the start of the narrow dirt track.

Elena took it and a lump grew in her throat. Señora Montalvo really needs me, she thought.

Without planning to, she squeezed her hand and the older woman smiled.

"You'll love the woods," she said. "The path we're on is a short cut to the main road. You know how the road curves around the hill." They walked a while and then she stopped by a large sycamore. "I know where we are," she said. "I know this place as well as I know my own hands. See the clearing over there by the cypress tree? You can see the coastline from there. Sometimes, even the island of Santa Catalina."

"It's a very pretty spot," Elena said as Ana started down the path again.

The spell of the woods was hard to resist: the spears of sunlight, dancing with mist; the echoes of rushing wings; the wonderful woodsy scent. Elena was sorry when they came to a short incline that led to the asphalt road. The little slope was ribbed with logs embedded in earth, forming footholds. Across from the road a stone building was almost hidden by the trees. It might have been lost except for a redwood sign that said "The China Cup," with an arrow pointing to it.

"Shall we cross?" Elena asked.

"Of course. We'll have a cup of tea before we return. The China Cup is a funny little shop. It's a tea room with antiques and a small grocery store on the side."

Elena went ahead of her. "Here, Señora Montalvo, take my hand."

"I'm Ana, remember?"

"I'll try," Elena said. She helped Ana find firm footing on each log that led to the road, and they crossed to The China Cup hand in hand. They walked through the small alcove that was the antique shop, its shelves shining with brass and silver and spilling over with potted plants. Ana showed her the corner that was the grocery store, pointing out the old cash register and antique scales, and then they went into the tea room.

They were seated at a table by a window that overlooked the road. A tiny blonde woman with a ruffled apron hurried to them. "Mrs. Montalvo! How good to see you. It's been such a long time. And what can I get you?"

After asking for a pot of tea and a basket of pastries, Ana leaned back against her chair and closed her eyes.

It was only for an instant, but in that instant Elena's mind raced with questions and speculations: What was wrong with Señora Montoya's eyesight? Was it caused by an illness? Maybe the walk was too tiring for her. I'll ask Doctor Montalvo when I see him another time, but I wonder when that will be. I haven't seen him since early yesterday. Is he gone? Well, even if he is, I certainly have to do what he told me. Later today, I have to help the boys with their school work. I hope they won't fight. I hope Carlos isn't teasing Mario too much. I hope...

"Here's your tea," the cheery little blonde said. "Enjoy."

Ana sat up and smiled. "I'm so glad you decided to stay with me, Elena," she said. "Lately, Salvador has become involved in a special project that takes him away a good deal."

"Is Doctor Montalvo gone now?"

"He's leaving tonight for a couple of days. David is coming to stay with me while he's gone. David's only ten miles away, but he has such a hectic schedule that he hasn't been home in weeks. When I called, he said he couldn't make it any sooner, but he promised he'd be here today." She leaned across the table and said in a confiding tone, "I didn't tell him about your being here. It was such a good chance for me to visit with him."

David. The boy in the photograph. According to Mrs. Addison, grown into "a strapping young man...handsome...not one of your wild ones." She was going to meet David, Ernesto Martel's son!

They finished tea and then they were outside, crossing the road to the planked slope.

Elena helped her companion onto the first log. "Wait there," she said, " I will come up ahead—"

The rest of her words were lost in a cry. A yellow car squealed around the curve in the road, scattering leaves and dust. It came so close to the hill that Elena scrambled up its side, clinging to the scrub growth.

"Elena!" Ana called. "Are you all right?"

"I'm all right," Elena said, and slid down to the road. "Scratched, dirty and still shaking, but all right. The saints were watching out for me."

"What happened?"

"That car almost hit me. The driver must be crazy. Else, why would he want to drive on the side of the hill?"

"Careless fool," the woman above her said. "I didn't see him, but I heard his tires screeching by."

Elena brushed leaves from her hair and wiped her face on her shirt sleeve. "Well, he's gone. From now on, I'll be more careful." She climbed up beside the older woman. "Here, take my hand."

Little by little as they went on, Elena's heart stopped racing. Her breathing returned to normal and she began to enjoy the walk again. At a juncture of two trails, Ana pointed to the right.

"Let's take this one back," she said. "It's long, but it's lovely. We'll be making a circle of about two miles around the hill to the house."

They turned sharply on to a path that led through a dense growth of trees. The afternoon sun sent occasional fingers of misty light through the leaves, giving the woods an unreal, painted look. Above them blue jays screeched and pigeons scattered in sudden rushes of wings, as if frightened. Later, ahead of them in a patch of sky, she saw a hawk swoop into a clump of cypresses. Now and then she thought she heard footsteps rustling the leaves behind them, but she told herself that the sounds were made by squirrels. Even so, she was glad when they came to a clearing.

Ana said, "Look up there. There's the house."

"I see it. On that hilltop." The sunlight caught the windows, and as she watched, the western side of the house seemed to become a face. The glittering panes were eyes, searching the ocean and the edges of the city below. Elena thought, what am I doing here? Why am I not down in the city finding my father? And as she walked beside Ana, she made a plan. She would figure out a way to get to Emerald Avenue. Someone there *had* to know her father.

They continued their climb. For all its steepness, it was not a hard walk. The trees now were more widely spaced, and broad shafts of sunlight slanted through them to piles of last year's cones and matted leaves. Soon they arrived at a back gate of the house and walked on a gravel path that took them by the garages. Ana led them along the kitchen and dining wing toward the front of the house.

Mrs. Addison was standing by the open kitchen door. "Mrs. Montalvo," she said, "I don't like to break into your afternoons, don't you know, but there's days when I have to. Do you have a speck of time for me?"

"You know I do, Bertha. I'll come into the kitchen." She pressed Elena's arm. "I'll see you at supper."

The walk that Elena had dreaded so much was over, and it was she, not Ana, who had had the near accident. Her mood was lighter as she walked to the front door. She had made a decision, and Doctor Montalvo had promised her time for "her own pursuits." Soon she would go down to the city and ask some questions.

When she rounded the corner of the house, she was so immersed in her thoughts that she almost missed the sleek yellow car parked on the gravel by the door. She stopped when she saw it. She was sure that was the car that had made her scramble up the hill like a frightened jackrabbit, and she didn't want to run into the driver. She was still mad. She went up the steps hesitantly and put her hand on the knob.

Before she could turn it, the door opened and she was face to face with the angry young man of the day before. "You!" she said, pushing by him into the entry hall.

An eyebrow rose. Instead of going out he closed the door and walked over to stand at the bottom of the stairs. "Is there someone you want to see here?" he asked.

"Not now. I'm going to my room," she said, struggling to keep her irritation hidden. What was *he* doing here again?

"Your room?"

"Yes. I live here."

"Really?" His black eyes narrowed. "Here?"

"Why not? And if that's your yellow car out there, you don't care where I live—or if. As far as you know, I might be lying dead on the road!"

"Was that you? Hey, I'm sorry. I was trying to avoid killing a squirrel. I circled back to apologize, but you'd disappeared."

She was aware of the softening of his voice, but she didn't care. She had had two uncomfortable run-ins with this man, and she was prepared to dislike him. "Fine," she snapped. "Now, if you will please move out of my way, I'll go upstairs."

"So you live here." There was a puzzled frown on his face. "Well, well, and how did that happen?"

She glared at him. "Why should I answer your questions? Just move over, please."

He shrugged and made a sweeping movement toward the stairs as he stepped aside. Then his frown changed into a broad smile. Elena could not understand the suddenness of that smile until she realized that it was not meant for her. He was looking over the balustrade to the center of the entry hall.

"There you are, mother," he said. "I've been looking all over for you."

Elena glanced over her shoulder. Ana was standing by the entry to the breakfast room corridor. "David, how nice! You're early."

Elena ran up the stairs, her face reddening, her eyes smarting with hot tears. How could she have been so stupid? Still, how could she have guessed that this man and the David that Mrs. Addison had described were one and the same? This David was handsome, yes, but that was where the similarity ended.

In her room she washed her face with cold water and plopped into the chair by the bay window, feeling miserable. Elena, she told herself, you have not one foot, you have two, in your mouth—and a sharp tongue, too. When are you going to learn to think before you speak? She huddled in the chair, dreading what Ana would say about her rudeness, wondering if there was anything she could do to make up for it, when suddenly a new thought hit her.

She stiffened and sat up. Something was wrong here, and it had nothing to do with her. Ana had said that David had not been home in weeks. Yes, that is what she had said. And David had been here only yesterday.

CHAPTER NINE

Elena pushed herself up from the chair and went into her brother's room. It was empty, but there was evidence that Carlos had been there. Three new textbooks and a notebook with a large "L" stamped on it were scattered on the bed, and Carlos' good pants were crumpled on the floor, right where he had stepped out of them. But he *had* changed. And she wondered why.

She looked at the books. One was bilingual, and she thought, good, Carlos will begin to learn English. Then she picked up the pants and hung them up.

Back in her room, she went to stand at the bay window. She was still embarrassed about the incident with David Martel and irritable about it. Breathing in the cool scent of the eucalyptus trees, she shook her shoulders and determined to rid herself of the uncomfortable feeling. What I should be doing, she told herself, is finding Carlos before *he* does something to embarrass me. Although I don't need help; I do well enough alone. Turning, she walked across the room to the hall door. But she didn't open it. Behind her, through the window, came a shout. "Hey, Carlos, get down! You'll hurt yourself!" It was Mario.

Elena hurried to the window in time to see Carlos shinny down the trunk of a eucalyptus tree. She smiled. Mario would soon learn that trees were her brother's other habitat.

Once on the ground, Carlos touched Mario's chest with his index finger and, motioning to the tree, said in Spanish, "Go on! You do it. It's easy."

Mario held back. "I can't. I'll tear my pants."

"What're you saying?" Carlos asked impatiently.

Mario pointed to a pants leg. Then he took the fabric between his fingers and pretended to tear it. "I'll tear my pants," he said again.

"Pants," Carlos said in English, and the word was as clear as the ring of a bell. *"Pantalones."*

"*Pantalones*," Mario repeated with a shy grin.

Carlos frowned and dug at the ground with the toe of his shoe. Elena knew that gesture. Her brother was planning something. Suddenly, Carlos raised his head and scanned the house. Then he motioned to Mario, and the two boys disappeared behind the trees.

Elena waited, wondering. When the boys reappeared, Carlos was without pants, his bare legs long and lean like a pair of saplings in the sunlight. Mario was zipping up Carlos' frayed jeans. "Neat," Mario said. "These are neat."

"*Andale*," Carlos said, again pointing at the tree. "Go on. It's easy."

Mario hugged the trunk of the tree and tried to shinny upward, but he could get no traction. After two or three tries he turned and shook his head fiercely. He was red-faced as he said, "I don't wanna climb trees."

Carlos laughed. "Dummy," he said in Spanish, "why did you put your shoes back on?" Mario looked as if he was about to cry. Carlos bent over and pointed to Mario's feet. "Shoos," he said in an attempt at English, "shoos." And then, "No shoos."

"O-o-oh." Mario ran his arm across his face, sat down on the ground, and proceeded to remove his leather-soled shoes. He grinned as he stood up barefooted and said, "Now?"

Carlos nodded vigorously. *"Andale."*

Mario hugged the tree trunk once more and, after a couple of rough starts, made it up to where the tree bent gracefully into a sturdy branch. He climbed out onto the branch and called, "Hey, Carlos, look at me!"

Carlos slapped at an insect on his leg and glanced up. "So?" he mumbled in Spanish. "I said it was easy."

Elena turned away from the window. Well, she had found Carlos, and he was doing a better job at getting along than she was. He had made friends with Mario. And she? How was she going to face Ana or her son?

The closer the time came, the more convinced she was that she didn't want to go down to dinner. But she couldn't get out of it. Doctor Montalvo had been firm about their eating the evening meal with the family. If it had been up to her, she would have gone without eating. As it was, she put on the loveliest of the long-sleeved shirts Ana had given her and the mid-calf gray skirt that Doctor Flores in Playa Blanca hated. "You're hiding those pretty legs again," he would say whenever she wore it. "Don't you want to make my patients happy?"

She glanced at the skirt in the mirror, wiped the top of her shoes, and gave her hair some additional brush strokes before calling Carlos away from Mario's room and the television set.

As they went down the stairs to supper, Carlos told Elena about his day at "*la escuela americana*." "That American school is good," he said seriously. "It is only the way they run it that is bad."

"And why is that bad?"

"Well, why do you think? Only one person there talks Spanish—and he is a teacher!"

"What a thing," she said. "And did *you* learn any English?"

"I learned to say 'cheequen.' That's what we ate for lunch."

"You are going to have 'cheequen' again. Mrs. Addison told me."

"Do I have to eat it?"

"Yes. And with a knife and fork."

"You are not my mother, Elena. You are just my sister. How come you always tell me what to do?"

"Because I raised you, remember? And because you will eat like old Pancho's ugly pig if I don't. Another thing, Carlos, for the sake of the saints and yours, don't talk too much."

She need not have worried. No one talked much at dinner except Mario and David. It was obvious that Mario was excited at having his older brother home, and he was full of questions. Through their talking she learned more about David. He was a student at Loyola Law School. He lived in town with a roommate named Stuart. His yellow car was a Porsche. He like basketball and baseball. He also liked his little brother. And another thing was clear. He had more patience with Mario than she did with Carlos.

A couple of times David tried to include Elena in the conversation, but each time Mario interrupted. She was just as glad. He's only being kind, she thought, and I'm such an open letter. He can tell I'm still uncomfortable. Every now and then, when he was looking the other way, she glanced across the table at him. In a crisp, open-collared blue shirt, he had lost resemblance to the tee-shirted young man she had bumped into twice before.

Doctor Montalvo, seated at the head of the table, ate hurriedly. Before the meal was over, he rose. "Forgive me, my dear," he said to Ana, "but I have telephone calls to make before I leave, and the time is getting short."

Ana stirred. She looked strained and pale as she said, "Do what you must. I understand."

David leaned back in his chair. "Flying again, Montalvo? On another chartered plane?"

Doctor Montalvo turned quickly, his hands pressed tightly against the table. His eyes were brilliant as he said, "Of course, David. My time is worth money."

"I'm sure it is," David said dryly. "But a chartered plane is worth money, too—a lot of it."

In the short, sharp silence that followed, Elena saw the lines deepen around Doctor Montalvo's mouth. He nodded curtly. "Indeed," he said, and turned to her. "Ana has a list of recommended driving schools. Call one and arrange for your lessons. As you know, we expect you to begin on Saturday."

Her eyes had been on his taut, veined hands. She looked up hastily and said, "Yes, I understand. I will." She would call first thing tomorrow. Yes. But that was tomorrow, and there was still this difficult evening to get through. Something was going on that she didn't like. She wished she could excuse herself and leave the table, too.

Sara brought in a tray with coffee and cups. She shot Elena a look as she placed the tray before Ana, and Elena thought, Sara doesn't like that I am eating in the dining room or that I have that lovely room. She doesn't like the way they are treating me altogether.

When Ana had served the coffee, she stood up. "I must talk to Salvador," she said, and then added vaguely, "about the fiesta. The rest of you, please enjoy dessert. It's your favorite, David. Mrs. Addison's banana cream pie."

As his mother left the room, David's eyes darkened and, for the briefest of instants, his face took on a helpless look. Despite the fact that the dessert had been announced as his favorite, he ate very little of the pie. Mario, however, gulped down every bit and pushed his chair away from the table.

"Hey!" he said to Carlos. "I have a new game in my room. Wanna see it? Come on, I'll beat you up there!"

Carlos shrugged and looked at Elena, a question in his eyes. But when Mario repeated, "Come on!" and tugged at his arm, he pushed his chair back and raced out of the dining room after him.

After the boys left, there was a long awkward silence. Elena wanted to say something clever, something to show that the incident in the hall hadn't bothered her, but she could think of nothing. She put down her fork. The pie on her plate was gone; not a bite was left to give her something to do. And her coffee was still too hot to drink. She took a sip of water and stared at the intricate "M" etched into the glass. Finally, David spoke.

"I should've explained who I was this afternoon. If I had, our first meeting might have gone better."

"That wasn't our first meeting," Elena said, and took another sip of water. She put the glass down with great care. "Don't you remember? We met yesterday in the entry hall."

David threw his hands in the air and let them fall on his lap with a loud whack. "Wouldn't you know it? Now I have two strikes against me." He was silent for a moment, then he said, "I'll appreciate it if you don't tell mother that you saw me here yesterday. Might upset her."

"Well, then, of course I won't." She's upset already, Elena thought and fought back an impulse to ask why. She stood up. "I have to go to work," she said. "Helping the boys. Excuse me, please." He nodded and she left the dining room without a backward glance, holding her head at what she told herself to be a nice, dignified level.

She found Carlos and Mario again watching TV. "Your television's too attractive, Mario. We'd better do the schoolwork in my room."

Later, after their homework was done, Mario brought in a Monopoly game and tried to explain it to Carlos, but Carlos did more shrugging than understanding. Almost immediately, arguments began.

"I'm not a referee," she told them, "only an interpreter, so forget the game. In any case, there's no time left for it tonight."

She was right. In just a few minutes Sara knocked at the door and said it was bedtime for Mario and that his mother was waiting to see him.

"It's bedtime for all of us," Elena said, smiling, but Sara didn't reply.

Carlos, contrary to his usual behavior, didn't argue about having to go to bed, but instead went into his room and started pulling off his clothes. "Elena," he said, "when are we going to find Papá?"

"Soon," Elena said firmly, "soon." She settled Carlos down and in a few minutes got into bed herself. Her sleep was restless, interrupted by awakenings. Close to dawn she heard the tentative chirping of birds and then slept again.

Birds were chirping above her in the woods as a yellow-wheeled car hurtled down a narrow dirt path. Its headlights beamed on a man who was running to escape it. "Papá!" she screamed. "Jump behind the trees!" He jumped, but the trees disappeared as he did, and he fell over the edge of a cliff, down, down, down to the needle-shaped buildings of the city below. And then she was rolling down an asphalt road. Over and over and around and around the hill she went until she heard the sound of water and came to a sudden stop at the edge of the ocean. David Martel was sitting on the sand. "Are you looking for someone?" he asked.

The dream stayed with her all morning and into the afternoon. Maybe it was because she had too much time on her hands. Ana and David were gone most of the day: Ana, to lunch and a concert with friends; David, to attend a lecture at school. They both returned in time for a dinner that was relaxed and pleasant. Ana was particularly light-hearted. Elena wondered if it was David's presence or Doctor Montalvo's absence that made her so.

That night Elena's sleep was dreamless. She awakened to find sunlight angling through the partially open drapes. The clock on the mantle told her that she had nearly overslept, but instead of sitting up, she stretched slowly. I'll make up the time, she told herself. And then, remembering: Besides, this is Saturday. I'm on my own until my driving lesson at ten o'clock. She swung her feet to the floor and pulled open the drapes. Carlos and Mario were splashing in the swimming pool. David, in swim trunks, was sitting on the diving board talking to them. What fun Carlos is having! It'll be hard to tear him away from here. But the sooner, the better. Today I'll start looking for my father.

At exactly ten o'clock she was sitting on the front steps, waiting for the instructor from the driving school. She hoped he would be a pleasant man because she was going to ask him to let her practice driving in traffic right away. She would suggest streets like the boulevard that La Fonda, the restaurant, was on, and others like Emerald Avenue.

A white Cadillac swung onto the gravel from the side of the house and stopped close to her. David, in jeans and white tee shirt, got out on the far side. He grinned as he walked around the front of the car toward her.

She said, "Good morning. For a moment I thought you were the man for my driving lesson."

"I am. Get in and I'll explain." He opened the car door.

She shook her head. "I can't. I'm waiting for the man from the driving school."

"He's not coming. They called. He can't be here till Monday."

"Oh," she said, and she knew her disappointment showed. She had built her hopes on this lesson, and now...

David looked amused. "I thought I'd give you your first lesson. I already cleared it with the lady of the house."

"Well," she said, "if Señora Montalvo says it's all right..." She stood up slowly and got into the car. He slid into the driver's seat, and the Cadillac moved smoothly through the open gates.

She was not certain what she felt, disappointment, annoyance, or even a kind of gladness as she buckled her seat belt and glanced at him. He drove silently, a touch of a smile on his mouth. He is as handsome as his father was, she thought, and he smiles like him. When she found herself wondering if his father had used the same musky after-shave that she could smell faintly right now, she forced her mind onto other things. "Can we begin the lesson now?" she said.

"On this hill? Not on your life. It's loaded with bad turns, including Dead Man's Curve. No, not here. We're going to a nice deserted road I know."

"I already know how to drive a car on a deserted road," she said. "That's where I learned, on an empty old road outside of Playa Blanca." He threw her an odd look and she spoke quickly. "What I need to learn is how to drive on busy streets... like the streets in the city."

He shot her another look. "You learned in Playa Blanca? In Mexico?"

She nodded. "But I can't drive here until I've had practice."

"That's for sure. All right, we'll go somewhere where you can get used to mother's car and the Los Angeles traffic."

"Good," she said, and added, "Do you know a street called Emerald Avenue?"

"Never heard of it."

"It's over that way," she said, waving her arm vaguely. "By a street called Lincoln."

"Lincoln I know," he said. "Everyone does."

The car hummed down the road, curving around the hill. Soon they left the wooded area behind. She began to catch frequent glimpses of the sea and in a matter of minutes they stopped at the traffic light that intersected the oceanside road.

David pulled the car to the curb and opened the glove compartment. He took out a street map and unfolded it. "Now," he said, "let's find out where Emerald Avenue is."

CHAPTER TEN

"Okay, I know where we're going," David said, and put the map away. He made a left turn at the signal and settled back to drive.

As they went by the hazy blue ocean, Elena felt more optimistic about finding her father. And underlying that optimism was gratitude. Right now she was grateful to David. He hadn't questioned why she wanted to go to Emerald Avenue; he was going there because she had asked him to. As she thought back to the last few days, she realized that many people had been kind to her, and her gratitude spread to others. Including Sylvia Lewis.

On the day before Elena left Playa Blanca, she had gone to say goodbye to Sylvia, the woman who had become her mentor and friend. Sylvia lived in a small house that was on the outskirts of Playa Blanca near the sand dunes and the sea. A five-foot wall enclosed not only the house but a large coral tree and a garden that Sylvia tended with loving discipline.

After locking up Doctor Flores' office for the last time, Elena walked slowly up the Calle Central toward her friend's home. She said a silent goodbye to the stuccoed shops and whitewashed houses she went by. First there was the Farmacia Argüelles, the small cluttered drug store adjacent to Doctor Flores' office. And next to that was Gordo's

Panadería, with yeast and sugar smells still coming through its open door. This was the place where she had met Sylvia more than ten years before, a tremulous child stepping in to translate for the confused American lady what Gordo was saying about the bread. In another few steps she went by an ice cream shop with a plastic penguin glued to its window. She had a compulsion to go in, to sit on one of the stiff metal chairs and ask for a pineapple ice just so she could watch old Señor Núñez shave the ice and pump the golden syrup over it once more. But there was no time for that.

She left the shops behind and with them the broken sidewalk. The street here was unpaved, the ground hard and rutted like her aunt's ancient washboard. There were a few scattered houses and then the dunes, and beyond them a broad expanse of white sandy beach and the clear ocean. Smells of cooking came from the houses. But except for the children playing in their yards, she saw no one.

She closed Sylvia's gate firmly, and as she turned, she heard her. "Elena, over here."

Sylvia was sitting on a bench in the shade of the coral tree. Her short gray hair was tied in a loosely knotted scarf and she was wearing a paint-daubed smock. "I know why you're here," she said, "and I hate it." She made room for Elena on the bench beside her.

Elena said, "I hate saying goodbye to you, too. But I belong with my father. Especially now."

"I don't like bringing this up again," Sylvia said, "but is it wise to go? You have your job here—oh, you'll find a better one—and you have friends. Los Angeles is a big city. What'll you do if you don't find your father?"

"I'll find him, Sylvia. He'll be there. He always has been."

"But something might've happened to him."

"I don't think so. He's a very capable man." Elena patted her friend's arm. "Anyway, I've already made up my mind."

"I knew that," Sylvia said. "But I thought I'd give it one more try." She dug in her pocket. "Here, take this. It's a letter to a friend of mine. Go to her if you find that you need help."

"I won't need help. I'll be all right."

"Take it," Sylvia had said. "For my sake."

Now, Elena glanced at David and thought, I wouldn't have a job or a place to live if it weren't for Sylvia.

When they turned onto Lincoln Boulevard Elena's optimism grew. She recognized La Fonda. The orange door of the restaurant was brilliant in the bright sunlight. The windows, too, sparkled. Juan Otero, a squeegee in one hand, a plastic pail in the other, was standing near the curb gazing with apparent satisfaction at the job he had just completed. Señor Otero knows my father, she thought. I have to talk to him again.

To David she said, "It's very nice of you. Bringing me down here."

"No big deal. Glad to do it."

"When do I start my lesson?"

"When we get to Emerald."

"But shouldn't I practice on streets like Lincoln, too? Driving for your mother is part of my job."

"I know." He looked mildly puzzled. "Funny you should've gotten the job. What made you apply?"

"I didn't."

"You didn't? What do you mean?"

"That I didn't apply for the job."

"Then how'd you end up with it?"

"Well, because Doctor Montalvo thought I was an applicant, only I wasn't. And then he told me I wasn't qualified because I didn't have a valid driver's license...and then..." She paused and frowned. "Then he turned right around and offered me the job. No, wait. I think it was after I showed him the letter from my friend, Sylvia Lewis, that he decided."

"*Sylvia Lewis*?" David made a sudden swing into a narrow street and stopped the car by a weed-grown empty lot. Broken bottles littered the ground, glinting green and amber in the sun. He stared at them for a while and then turned toward her, his shoulder pushed against the door. "Sylvia Lewis is *your* friend?"

"Yes," she said. "Is there something wrong with that?"

David, she noted, had the courtesy to look chagrined. "No, of course not," he said in an apologetic tone. "I was just surprised. So the letter's the reason Montalvo gave you the job."

"I think so. And it's a good thing. I have to work, you see. Especially since I'm having trouble finding my father." In a calm, practical voice she told him about her first day in Los Angeles.

When she was through, David said, "I can see why you wanted to come back to this neighborhood." He straightened himself out on the seat and reached for the ignition. With his hand over the key, he turned and said, "Look, María Elena, I..."

She stopped him. "If you'll say Elena, I'll say David."

He grinned and started again. "Look, Elena, I'm not trying to move into your act, but...well, maybe I could be of help to you in looking for your father. Ninety per cent of being a private eye is asking questions and looking up records, and what else does a lawyer do? So, if you want a hand, I'm willing."

It was hard for Elena to answer him. A plain old yes, thank you, was in order, but she was afraid that the words would come out in a croak. "I want a hand," she said finally. "Thank you."

"Okay then, let's go." He started the engine. "Emerald's just around the corner." When the car came to a stop at the curb near the numbers 1123 David said, "Where to?"

"Over there," she said, motioning to a white house next to her father's address.

Two small boys were playing with an automobile tire behind the wobbly picket fence. When David and Elena walked into the yard, they called, "*¡Mamá, Mamá, ven acá!*" A woman holding a baby appeared behind the screen door. Elena told her quickly that she was looking for her father, that he had lived next door, and the woman shook her head sadly.

"I'm sorry," she said, and went on to explain that she had lived in this house only two months. That the only people she had seen next door were the woman with the straw-colored hair and her husband. No, no Gómez family. And, no, she had never heard of Miguel Vargas. Ah-h-h, but one moment. The woman's forehead puckered. Across the street, yes, right over there, lived an *americano* who always spoke kindly to the boys and who appeared to know everyone on the block. For a certainty he would be able to help her and the young man.

"*Gracias*," Elena said.

"*Sí. Gracias*," David echoed her and she turned to him in surprise. He grinned. "Anyone can say, '*gracias*.'" He pushed open the stubborn picket gate and held it for her. " Come on."

They headed toward a faded turquoise house across the street. Pots of straggling geraniums stretched across the front porch and two graying bath towels hung over the railing. She knocked on the wooden frame of a screen door and, almost instantly, a thin, balding man appeared on the driveway at the end of the porch.

"What d'ya want?" he asked as he leaned on the railing, a mud-caked trowel in his hand.

Elena hurried down the steps. "Do you know Miguel Vargas?" she asked. "I'm his daughter. I'm looking for him."

He looked at her intently, but said nothing.

"He lived over there with the Gómez family," she said, and waved across the street at the two-story house.

The man put the trowel down, scratched his thinning hair, and said, "Yep, I knew him."

"You did? That's wonderful!"

"He's your father, eh?"

"Yes. Yes, he is," she said, and started toward him. "Do you know where I can find him?"

"Nope."

"Oh." Elena stopped in midstep. "Well, can you tell me when you last saw him?"

"Been a long time."

"Like a few weeks? A few months?"

The man shrugged.

David came up behind her. "How long would you say, sir?"

"Why the questions?" The man's eyes narrowed. "He in trouble?"

"Oh, no!" Elena said. "It's only that my brother and I came here to live with him and we can't find him."

The man shook his head slightly, picked up the trowel and started to turn away. She spoke quickly.

"The Gómez family. Do you know where they went?"

"Yep," he said. And then before she could ask, "Mexico."

Elena fought back her disappointment. "Then I can't talk with them."

The man scratched his head once more and his face worked in thought. "You his daughter, eh? Might as well tell you. There's been others with questions."

"There were?" she asked. "Who?"

"Men. Couple of 'em. Called it business. Might've been. Might've been. Wearing Sunday clothes, both of them."

"What kind of business?" David asked.

"Didn't say."

"What *did* they say?" David insisted.

"Don't rightly remember." With an indignant look at David, the man swung around and walked down the cracking cement driveway. As he turned the corner of his house, he looked over his shoulder and grumbled, "Nothing. Don't remember nothing."

Elena stared at the corner of the house and thought, there are only two people who say they know my father, this man and Juan Otero at La Fonda. Well, I won't let go of either one of them. It doesn't matter that they haven't seen him for a long time. At least, they've seen him.

David said, "What next?" and she pointed to the neighboring house.

They knocked at three more doors. No one had heard of Miguel Vargas, nor had anyone seen two men asking about him.

At the car she said, "I wonder who those men were? I've got to know."

"Don't worry about it."

"Maybe I should talk to more neighbors. There must be someone who can tell me something."

"Leave it for another day."

"It won't be easy to come back another day."

"On your days off? Why not? Once you learn to drive in this traffic, you'll be okay."

Her face grew hot. "The driving! I'm sorry. I completely forgot!"

"There's plenty of time," he said as he opened the car door for her. "Get behind the wheel and we'll get started." He slid into the passenger's seat. "If you're a good student, I'll buy you lunch."

"I'll be a good student," she said. "And I know exactly the restaurant I would like to go to."

For an hour and a half she learned about power steering, power brakes, directional signals, traffic signs and what David called "defensive driving." At the end of that time, according to David, she was ready to chauffeur him to the restaurant of her choice. With his help she found Lincoln Boulevard and brought the Cadillac to a halt by La Fonda.

With a shaky sigh of relief she handed David the keys. "This isn't Playa Blanca," she said. "All those cars! Where is everybody going?"

"Hey, lady," David said, "this is the big time. This is the city. Crazy, isn't it?"

The restaurant was crowded, but they found an empty booth near the kitchen. Elena kept turning around, hoping to catch a glimpse of Juan Otero, but all she saw were two busy waitresses. David and she sat patiently for what seemed a long time. Finally, she heard a rustling sound beside her. Luisa, wearing a red-tiered skirt and white blouse, stood by their booth.

"What can I get you?" she said without looking at them.

"How about a couple of menus?" David said.

Luisa gave David a long, appraising look. "You mean you don't have any? Now isn't that too bad. I'll get them." She moved idly toward the front of the cafe.

When she returned, Elena said, "Luisa, hello. Remember me? I'm Elena Vargas."

"Oh, it's you," Luisa said with apparent surprise. "What're you doing back again? Looking for more help? What happened? Did they kick you out of that fancy place?"

David, shaking his head in disbelief, said, "We came for lunch."

"And I came to talk to your father," Elena added, ignoring Luisa's acid remarks. "I hope he's here."

"He'd better be," Luisa said, "or you don't eat. What're you gonna order?"

Luisa served them. While they ate she hovered near the booth, glancing first at Elena, then at David. She wants to say something, Elena thought. I wish she'd do it and go away. Finally, while refilling their coffee cups, Luisa spoke.

"Hey, you, Elena," she said, "don't be in a hurry to leave, huh? I want to talk to you."

Elena looked at the clock on the wall. "I don't have much time," she said. "I have to get back because of my brother. Besides, I want to talk to your father."

"It won't take forever," Luisa said. "Just a minute or two."

David stood up. "I'll take care of the check and wait in the car." He hesitated. "That is, if you want me to, Elena."

"Hey, you don't have to leave," Luisa said. "We can talk in the girls' room. We're not going to be all afternoon."

"Girls' room? You mean the bathroom? Of course not."

Luisa shrugged. "Suit yourself. But I want to talk to you alone."

"Okay, Elena?" David asked, and when she nodded he walked over to the cash register.

When David was gone, Luisa slid into the seat he had left. She leaned across the table and, lowering her voice, said, "Are you from Playa Blanca?"

"Yes."

"I thought so. The day I met you I must've been half-asleep, because I didn't even hear what your name was. Sure, sure, you told me, but it was awfully early, remember."

"My name is María Elena Vargas."

Luisa made a wry face. "Sure, I know that now. It finally sank in. That's what I want to talk to you about."

"What silliness is this? Why would you want to talk to me about my name?"

"Why don't you just shut up and listen!" Luisa hissed. "You're still looking for your old man, aren't you?"

"Yes, but what has..."

"Let me finish!" Luisa got up, looked into the kitchen, returned and slid into the booth. "I know something you'll want to hear. It has to do with a man my father hid in the storeroom. Maybe a couple of months ago. He must've thought everybody was asleep because it was late. But I wasn't. I came downstairs and listened. The man in the storeroom was running away from something, and he was scared. Boy, was he scared!"

"That couldn't be my father," Elena said, shaking her head.

"I'm not saying it was," Luisa said. "All I'm saying is that man had a daughter coming from Playa Blanca. And her name was María Elena."

CHAPTER ELEVEN

Elena felt the blood rush to her cheeks. Her father! It had to be her father. And yet it was difficult to imagine him hiding in a dark storeroom, shaking with fear.

Luisa was staring at her, a knowing smile on her face. Elena stared back. Except for the slight twitch at a corner of Luisa's mouth, Elena might have thought that Luisa was completely relaxed, maybe even a little bored with the situation. She felt a flare-up of intense irritation. Luisa, she guessed, was probably sixteen. How could she have developed so much hardness in such a few years?

A fruit fly was skittering across the remains of food on Elena's luncheon plate. Luisa moved suddenly and shoved the plate to the end of the table. "You gonna sit there forever?" she asked harshly. "Didn't you hear what I told you?"

"I heard. I just don't understand."

"Shit! What's to understand? You know that was your old man."

"It couldn't be. Your father said he hadn't seen him in over four months."

"So? That's his problem."

"Well," Elena said, sliding across the seat, "I'll ask him about it. Where is he?"

"He won't tell you anything."

"How can you say that? If he talked with my father, he'll tell me."

"Try him if you want," Luisa said. "Go ahead. He's in the kitchen, and he's not even busy."

Elena jumped up and pushed the swinging door into the kitchen. She paused there, looking for Señor Otero. Huge pans and kettles hung above an island counter in the center of the kitchen and beyond it, by a far wall, two young men in white aprons talked and laughed above the clatter of the dishes they were washing. At the side of the room Juan Otero was bent over a griddle, wiping it clean.

"Señor Otero," she called, "may I talk with you, please?"

"In just a minute," he said without looking up.

"Of course," Elena said. "I'll wait." And then she added, "I'm María Elena Vargas. Remember? I was here a few days ago." He raised his head and looked at her, and Elena thought she saw a frown come and go on his face.

"Yes, I remember you," he said, and walked toward her, his plump hands busy with a towel.

When he was near she said, "When I was here before, señor, you said you didn't know anything about my father. But now Luisa says you talked to him in your storeroom just a month or so ago. If you did, isn't there something you can tell me?"

Juan Otero turned away and laid the towel on a counter behind him. He faced her again, his head moving from side to side as he sighed. "That girl and her stories. She tries the patience of the saints."

She does that, all right, Elena thought. "And there's more," she said. "Luisa says that the man with you, my father, spoke about a girl from Playa Blanca, a girl called María Elena."

"My daughter said that?" Juan Otero's smooth round face was furrowed into an expression of pain, and for one terrible moment Elena thought that he was going to cry. He reached into his pocket for a large white handkerchief and blew his nose before he said, "Señorita, I told you I could tell you nothing about your father. If I could, I would."

"But what about the storeroom? And the man there? What is Luisa talking about?"

Juan Otero spread his hands helplessly. "Who can say? My daughter has much imagination. As for me, there is nothing I can tell you except that I believe you will find your father. And until that time, if there is anything I can do for you, please call on me."

She had a compulsion to reach out to him, to comfort him. But she realized that he was trying to comfort her. The two men at the sink were quiet now, throwing looks in their direction, so she lowered her voice as she said, "Well, then, tell me this. Has there been anyone here asking about him?"

"Ah, yes. Several of my customers. As I told you, he ate here often."

"No, no, señor," she said. "I don't mean that. Strangers, I mean. Two men. Two men in business suits maybe."

"So many people come and go in this restaurant. It would be hard to recall. I'm sorry." His shoulders drooped as he walked to the swinging door and held it open. "I'm very sorry."

Elena was touched by his obvious distress. He would help her if he could; she felt sure of that. The swinging door fell into place behind her as she walked into the restaurant. Across the room at a table by the front window, a man and woman looked up at her and then returned to their eating. In the booth near the kitchen, Luisa, slumped in the seat again, was looking at her through half-closed eyes.

"Satisfied?" she said, and the word spit out like the hissing of an angry cat.

"Yes, I am." Luisa was waiting to enjoy her disappointment, waiting to hear her plead for information. All right, Luisa, she thought, you'll have a long wait. She said, "Your father knows nothing."

"Hah!" Luisa sat up. "You didn't really buy that, did you?"

"Buy that? What does that mean? I believed him, if that's what you want to know."

"You're dumb, you know?" Luisa said blandly. "Dumber than I thought. I told you he wouldn't admit anything."

"I know you did. Goodbye." She started for the door.

"Elena!"

Elena stopped and said, "No, Luisa, I don't want to hear more."

"Yes, you do," she drawled. "The man I saw with my father was about...oh, about five feet ten. Husky, you know, built like a football player. They only had one candle for light, but I could see enough. He had lots of dark hair that's getting gray, and thick eyebrows, almost bushy."

Elena swung around. Her hands were shaking. She's describing my father! How could she if she hadn't seen him? "You *do* know something, don't you? What is it? Tell me."

"Sure, I will. But before I do, I want money. Like fifty dollars."

It took a moment for Luisa's words to make sense. Luisa wanted to *sell* her what she knew for fifty dollars. A knot tightened in her stomach as she stared at the slight, wispy-haired girl in the full red skirt and thought, a week ago I did not know her, a week ago I had never heard of her... Angry tears burned her eyes. She clenched her hands, and the fury that had begun with the knot in her stomach spilled out in words, words that she hardly recognized as her own.

"What do you think, huh, Luisa? That I am one of your little girl friends? One you can talk into doing whatever you want? Well, I'm not! I don't need you. If my father was in that storeroom, I'll find out. It may be a while, but I'll find it out!"

Luisa's face colored and her huge eyes widened. But she recovered her confident look almost immediately. "Maybe you will, and maybe you won't," she said. "Just don't wait too long. When you've got the money, come back."

Elena shook her head. "You don't hear very well, Luisa. I'm not giving you a single cent." She rushed down the room to the door. Outside she leaned against the wall of the building, trying to calm herself. But the noisy skirmishes of the cars on the street and the inquisitive stares of people passing by just served to feed her fury. She walked toward the car.

David was standing beside it, looking at her intently. "I was about to suggest that you drive us back to the house," he said, "but I don't think I will. You look pretty upset."

"I am."

"Anything I can do?"

"No. No, there's nothing anyone can do!" She got into the car, slammed the door and said, "That Luisa! I'm all mixed up. I don't know who to believe. And I won't give her money. Even if she described my father. And how? Where could she have—oh, Elena, use your head. The restaurant. He ate there. So she made it all up. All lies. But wait! The thing about Playa Blanca and..."

"Whoa, there," David said, raising one hand from the wheel. "If you finish your sentences, maybe I'll know what you're talking about."

"Sorry," Elena said. "I'm not making sense, am I? More like the babblings of an idiot."

"You don't sound like an idiot. You sound as if you're about to explode."

"I am, "Elena said, and told him about the talks with Luisa and Juan Otero. "I don't know what to think," she finished.

He nodded and drove for a while lost in thought. He's preoccupied with something far away, she thought. He must be tired of this. After all, he just met me, and all I've done is ask favors and talk, talk, talk about myself and my problems! She said, "All I've done today is whine. I'm sorry about that."

"Don't be," he said quickly. "I was just thinking about what you told me. Suppose you gave that conniving Luisa the money she wants, what then? Would you believe her? And suppose you did. That would mean that Juan Otero wasn't telling the truth. And why would he lie to you? What's the pay off for him?"

"I don't know," Elena answered pensively. "He seems like such a good man. I hate to think he's lying. And yet..." She left the words hanging limply.

"Well," David said, "this line of thinking is getting us nowhere. Let's try another direction. Do you remember anything at all, Elena, that might give you a clue as to where your father might be, what he might be doing? A telephone call, a message to your aunt, some kind of communication."

"The letters he wrote me. But I told you about them. There's nothing in them."

"Are you sure?"

"Yes, but I'll read them again. I've read them so many times I almost know them by heart."

"Something else, then. Could be something simple, something that seems unimportant."

She thought for a while, frowning. "I have an envelope," she said, "a sealed envelope that my father asked me to hold for him. But he gave that to me years ago."

"I'd have a look at what's inside if I were you."

"I'm not supposed to open it," she said. "It's not even addressed to me."

"Whose name *is* on it?"

"It has no name. Only the word 'Tamaulipas.'"

He threw her a swift sidelong glance.

She explained, "Tamaulipas is a state in Mexico."

"I know. I'd open that envelope if I were you."

"I'll think about it," she said.

They rode on in silence. The car soon left the ocean behind, twisting up the hill, taking the curves in a series of zigzags that were more and more abrupt. At every curve the tires squealed in seeming complaint. She had been so involved in her thoughts that she had not noticed the change in the way David was driving, but when she did, she looked at him in surprise.

He was frowning, his eyes narrowed on the sun-splattered asphalt. His light mood was gone. He seemed oblivious of her as he stared in angry concentration at the road ahead. The Cadillac swung to the left, narrowly missing the bumper of the car in front of them. David brought the big car back into the right-hand lane and straightened it without a comment. But in a moment he muttered, "Where do you fit in?"

"What?" Elena gasped. "What do you mean? I already told you how I came to be here."

There was a long pause. Then he shook his head and exhaled. "I didn't mean to say that. I thought I was just thinking it."

"But why were you even thinking it?"

"I'm not sure. It has to do with my stepfather. I don't like much what he does."

"Like hiring me?"

"Yes. Like hiring you. There's something fishy about that."

"What's fishy? *What*?"

"Damn it, Elena, I'm not sure about that either." They had turned onto Gray Ridge Drive, and the car moved quickly through the meadow toward the gates. "Look," David said, "if I explain any more, I'll be disclosing family matters, and I'd better not do that. Okay?"

"Okay," she said, but reluctantly. She wished he would explain. What was wrong with her working for his mother?

He brought the car to a stop by the front door, cut the engine and turned toward her with a smile. "Friends?" he said, extending his hand.

She took it. "Friends," she said, a little hesitantly. What was all this? She had seen David only three or four times, and on each of those times he had either been exploding with anger or driving dangerously. True, he had been kind to her today, and she appreciated it, but she couldn't let her appreciation get tangled up with worrying about his words or actions. Her worries had to do with her father, not with a temperamental person like David.

She pushed her thoughts aside and returned to where she was, sitting in the car beside the temperamental person. He was still holding her hand. Quickly, she drew it away.

CHAPTER TWELVE

Elena got out of the car, and, at that moment, Carlos came racing around the corner of the house.

"Elena, Elena, Mario's gone!" he called in Spanish. "He's run away!"

"Is anyone looking for him?" she asked.

"How can they?" Carlos said, extending his hands in an explanatory gesture. "Nobody knows where he is."

David looked at her with a question, and when she explained what Carlos had said, he laughed. "That makes sense. But I bet I know where he is. He has a hiding place in the woods. Come on, Carlos, let's go get him."

Elena watched them disappear around the corner of the house. As they did, a bleak sadness touched her. It was a short-lived feeling, but it lasted long enough to rouse an unhappy memory.

It was in Playa Blanca on the day her aunt and she had argued about her father that she had first felt the same kind of chilling emptiness. "Your father's forsaken you," her aunt had said grimly. "I knew the day would come." Then, without interrupting the rhythm of her creaking wooden rocker, her aunt had gone on complaining of the difficulties of raising her own four children. Elena barely heard her. She had been struggling with the unfamiliar feelings.

Now, as she went up the steps and into the house, her forehead was creased into a thoughtful frown. For a reason that was not clear, those feelings had echoed today. Inside the door she paused, looking with longing up the stairs. If only she could go to her room. Sit quietly. Figure out what more to do about finding her father. Maybe she should go to the police. Still, the two officers had thought he would return soon. Maybe in a city as immense as this one, such things were common. In Playa Blanca everyone knew who went where, and when, and why. There, an unexplained disappearance was cause for worry. She had to decide, too, what to do about Luisa. But this was not the time. Ana was expecting her.

The door to the plant room was slightly open, and she slipped in quietly. Ana was talking on the phone. When she was through, Elena said, "David's gone to get Mario. He knows where he is."

Ana said, "I'm sure he does. Mario's always running off to the woods. Sit here, Elena, I want to talk with you about our fiesta."

She took the chair Ana indicated and said, "Mrs. Addison said something about a fiesta. Will it be soon?"

"In exactly one week. We call it the Fiesta de Mayo. It's a tradition by now. Salvador started it the year we were married to introduce his students to some Mexican customs. There will be typical food, music, entertainment."

Elena nodded, remembering Doctor Montalvo's typically Mexican study. It seemed he not only surrounded himself in his culture, he wanted everyone to have a taste of it.

Ana sighed. "It's a lovely party, but it's grown out of hand, especially this year. The invitation list was so long. I wonder, Elena, if you could put together a piñata for the children?"

"If you will provide a clay pot and paper, I think I can. But, remember, it won't be as fancy as the ones you buy."

"No matter. Let the boys help you make it. Salvador will be pleased. You can work on it in the playroom just below us."

"That room? Doesn't Doctor Montalvo's assistant use it?"

The vague look appeared on Ana's face. "Of course," she said at last. "Well, then, use the workroom next to the garages. Mr. Addison will make room. Now, let's go on with our book, shall we?"

The afternoon had grown late, and waning daylight softened the colors of Elena's room when she finally returned to it. Carlos was piecing together a jigsaw puzzle on a board on the floor. She said, "I see you found Mario. Where was he?"

"It is not right to tell you, Elena. That is a secret place, that place of Mario's."

"Well, then don't tell me," she said sharply, and realized that she was tired, and that she was angry, and that she had sounded like a child.

Carlos picked up the board with the puzzle and carried it into his room. When he returned, he angled toward the door and said, "Mario is waiting for me downstairs."

"Are you going through the house?"

"I'm going to the kitchen."

"Well, use the back stairs, the ones that end by the breakfast room."

"But they're dark!"

"Not if you turn on the light at the top, silly."

This time she was glad to be left alone. She wanted to sort out the jumble of facts that was crowding her mind. Juan Otero's strange behavior. David's change of mood. And Ana. Lots of things happened to people's eyes. She had seen that in Doctor Flores' office. But there was something strange about Ana's problem. It was as if she drew a curtain over her eyes at times. Then there were the newspapers and the sealed envelope. They both said Tamaulipas. Was it really just coincidence?

She got up and pulled the envelope from beneath the clock. The paper was yellowed, the black ink, faded. It had lain at the bottom of her clothes drawer for years, and she had never been tempted to open it. Nor was she now, except for the fact that David had thought she should. She ran her fingers thoughtfully over the ancient envelope. And then with sudden decision, she slipped her thumbnail under the flap. At that moment the door behind her swung open and Carlos came into the room.

"Señora Montalvo wants you," he said, catching his breath. "She says to come right now. She says to bring a sweater. We're eating by the swimming pool, and David's going to cook the meat!"

"I'll be right there," she said, and waited for the door to close behind Carlos before she put the envelope away.

Minutes later she went down the outside staircase. When she saw the group centered in the U made by the two wings of the house, her mood lightened. Carlos and Mario were scuffling on the lawn. Ana sat at an orange umbrella table talking to David, a wine glass in her hand. And David, a long fork in his hand, was arranging steaks over a glowing charcoal fire. He looked up, saw her and smiled, but went on talking with his mother.

Feeling suddenly shy, suddenly unnecessary, Elena circled the pool to a wooden love seat that was sheltered by a bank of azaleas and a wall of oleanders. It was a lovely little corner, almost private, and she sat there until David said, "Hey, these steaks are ready. Where's Elena?"

Later, they drank coffee in the library. As soon as she could, Elena herded Carlos and Mario upstairs, leaving Ana and David sitting before the library fire. In her own room, watching the boys play a loud game of checkers, she was left with a flattened feeling.

She had been part of a happy group at dinner. David had described her driving lesson, telling of catastrophes that might have occurred had he not twisted the wheel this way or that, and provoking Elena to deny loudly and then burst into laughter. It had been a happy party, but once in the library, her mood had changed. She had sat stiffly staring at the paintings and tapestries lining the east wall. This was where Ernesto Martel had sat with his wife and son. This was a world outside her own. She did not belong, no matter how kind David had tried to be. Mario's shout brought her back to the present. "He can't jump two squares at a time! Can he, Elena?"

The minutes dragged as she waited for the boys' bedtime, but, finally, a knock came at the door. When she opened the door, she found not Sara, but David standing there.

"I came to ask you to go for a walk in a little while. Do you want to?"

"Yes," she said, "that'll be nice. As soon as Carlos is asleep."

"In half an hour?" When she nodded, he said, "Meet me at the pool then."

She closed the door and stared across the room, wondering at her feelings. Whatever they were, her dejected mood was gone.

It took most of the half hour for Carlos to fall asleep. She sat in her room waiting, forcing herself to stay, knowing that if she looked in on her brother he would start chattering. Finally, she allowed herself a look, and he was asleep, curled into a tight bundle under the blankets.

Outside, only the night lights were on, and she stood by the balcony railing for a moment and looked up at the sky. There *were* stars up there. Not the dense pearly netting of stars that hung over Playa Blanca, but a handful that winked down at her as if to say, "Here we are, Elena. We came along, too."

As she neared the pool, David stepped out of the shadows. "Come on," he said, reaching for her hand. "I have something to show you." When they came to the beginning of the path that Ana had called a short cut, she guessed where they were going. David said, "It's okay. There's a path here. And, besides, I know these woods..."

"Like your own two hands," she said, quoting Ana.

"Just about, but I brought along a flashlight anyway. And we're not going far."

She said nothing as David led the way on the trail she had taken with his mother. When they reached the sycamore by the fallen tree, he snapped off the flashlight. From the clearing in which they stood, she could see the coastline stretching to the south like a sequined velvet ribbon. Light-dotted buildings studded the higher ground, and here and there in the sky above them, the red and yellow lights of aircraft blinked.

David put the flashlight on the ground between them as they sat on the log. He said, "Isn't that something? I wanted you to see it at night, but it's great in the daytime, too. When I was a kid, I spent hours here daydreaming."

"Did any dreams come true?"

"Some," he said. "Like the day that you showed up. I always wanted to see you again."

"*Me*? What are you talking about?"

"Don't you remember? We played together on that beach in Playa Blanca."

Elena thought of the photograph on Doctor Montalvo's desk, the photograph of a younger Ana and a smiling boy. That must have been Playa Blanca, she thought. That must have been my beach! That's why it seemed so familiar. A feathery sensation swept along her spine. Memory stirred.

She was eight or nine. The day had been bright and sunny as she sat on the sand watching her cousins, Trini and Raúl, chase a boy, a stranger, along the curling white edges of the ocean. The boy swung inland, racing by her, exploding sand into her face. He had stopped. "I'm sorry," he said. And that was when Raúl caught him. "If you like shells, play with her!" Raúl shouted, shoving him to the ground. "Just leave us alone!" And for the rest of that week the boy had hung around her, maybe because she could talk English, maybe because she liked shells.

Now, Elena shook her head incredulously. "David, are you The Magician? Are you Merlin?"

"I could have been Arthur," David said matter-of-factly, "but Merlin always interested me more."

She grabbed for the flashlight and pointed it at his face. He grinned and blinked and put his arms over his eyes as she said, "You are! You were!"

"It took you long enough to remember me, even if it has been over ten years. Now put that thing down."

She flipped off the light. "But I only knew you for a week or so. And no one told me your name was David. You knew me because you had clues: my name, Playa Blanca, Sylvia Lewis..."

"And your face. It's the same, only prettier. But how could you possibly forget the guy who ruined that shell collection of yours?"

"Easy," she said, laughing. "What dumb kids we were! You really persuaded me that a magician could not possibly drop them, and I let you juggle them. Five at a time, right?"

"Don't exaggerate. Three."

"Well, five or three, I shouldn't have forgotten you. Not when you remembered the girl who gave you a black eye."

"Yeah. That wasn't nice, Elena."

"Nice? Look who's talking. You'd broken my shells!"

"Well, anyway, it wasn't much of a fight. You ran."

"I know."

"Don't tell me you were scared?"

"What else? You looked awfully big then."

"Well, I'm bigger now."

"But you don't frighten me anymore. I know now that you can't turn me into a frog."

"Just in case I have," he said, and leaned over and kissed her.

It was a quick kiss, just long enough to make her hungry for more.

"Don't we have this backwards?" she said. "If you want to be a prince, shouldn't I kiss you?"

When they stood up to go, David squeezed her hand and she left it in his as they walked back to the house. He said good night at the bottom of the balcony steps and went across the lawn to the other wing of the house.

She went up the steps slowly. David had kissed her, and his kisses had been warm and sweet. Merlin, The Magician. She grinned as she looked up at the winking stars. Yes, the night did seem to be touched with magic.

CHAPTER THIRTEEN

It was after midnight by the time Elena fell asleep. She dreamed that David and she were running along the seashore. It was a happy dream, one she didn't want to leave. When she heard footsteps and muffled voices coming through the open window, she groaned. She floated near awareness, refusing to give up sleep. Then, abruptly, she was awake and looking at the digital clock on the bedstand. It was five after three.

She was out of bed, pulling a light sweater around her shoulders before she fully realized what she was going to do. She walked to the balcony doors, opened them cautiously, and slipped outside. The woods were veiled in a thin gray mist. Except for the sound of moisture dripping from the boughs nearby, the night was still. But she was sure she had heard other sounds. She moved quietly along the balcony to the head of the stairs and, holding on to the stucco wall, peered around the corner. A circle of light moved on the slope of grass that led to the rooms on the lower level. A flashlight. She made out two people walking clumsily together. They were carrying a large object between them as they struggled up the grassy incline. The circle of light shifted and jumped wildly on the shrubbery near the house, finally stopping on the door to the playroom. She stared transfixed as they lowered the bulky object to the ground and stepped to the door, one man holding the light while the other bent over the lock. Thieves, she thought. I've got to let Ana know, or David. But where are their rooms? As she debated on what to do, the flashlight beam circled the patio and brushed the bottom of the staircase. She pulled her head back and pushed against the wall. When the beam stopped searching, she glanced around the corner once more. Silhouetted in the lighted doorway of the playroom was Jim Donald. He and the other man, whose back was toward her, lifted a square wooden box into the room. Almost immediately, they turned off the light. But not quickly enough to hide the face of the second man. It was Doctor Montalvo.

Her tightened muscles unwound, her breathing slowed down, and she shook her head impatiently. She had been making a mystery out of nothing. Doctor Montalvo was home. Obviously, he was taking care not to awaken his family, and here she was, prying on him and inviting a runny-nosed cold. With another impatient shake of her head, she turned and went inside.

Even with the interruption to her sleep, Elena awakened early the next morning. She was glad for the extra time. For a reason that her mind avoided, she was dressing slowly and carefully. And very particularly. She had torn off the second blouse she had tried on and was pulling on the third when Carlos, who had been waiting for her in the hall, pounded on the bedroom door again.

He looked at the blouses scattered on the bed and said, "How many shirts do you now have, Elena? Too many, eh? I want breakfast before you put on another one."

When Carlos and she arrived in the breakfast room, Ana and Mario were at the table. "Good morning," Elena said, and looked with disappointment at the empty chairs.

Ana said good morning and added, "David had an early-morning errand. He'll be back before noon."

"Oh." Elena busied herself with the food. Ana had known immediately that it was David she was looking for. Back at the table she unfolded her napkin and searched for something casual to say. "Doctor Montalvo must be tired from his trip."

"Salvador?" Ana said amiably. "He isn't home yet. I don't expect him till tonight."

"Oh," Elena said again, feeling stupid. She was certain that that one syllable had given her feelings away for the second time.

In her room after breakfast, she stood by the open balcony doors, frowning at the memory of what she had seen during the night. Could she have been mistaken about seeing Doctor Montalvo? No, the light had been full on his face. And yet Ana had said... Elena shrugged irritably. There was sure to be a simple explanation for Doctor Montalvo's actions. And whether there was or not, it was certainly none of her business. She had concerns of her own.

Like the second thoughts she was having today about opening her father's envelope. It was sealed and he had said, "Take care of this for me." Not, "You can look at it if you become curious." Of course, the circumstances were unusual. More than unusual, Elena told herself, grimacing. The circumstances are not good. And before they get any worse, I'd better do something about it. With that thought prodding her, she pulled the envelope from beneath the clock and sat on the bed to open it.

When she did, she found two yellowed, folded papers inside. She pressed them out carefully. The first was a letter. The second, a printed sheet with signatures that she recognized to be a deed for land in the Mexican state of Tamaulipas.

The letter was addressed to "My first-born son, Miguel." It was from her grandfather! He had died when she was seven, but she remembered him well: a big man with gentle hands and laughing eyes. "My son," the letter said, "you know me for a practical man, one who does not easily give way to fantasy or wishful thinking. For that reason, and others (to be honest, mainly, procrastination), I have not explored the desert land my own father left me." I shouldn't be reading this, Elena thought, but went on when she saw "...that land will be yours when I die, and with it, a legend of riches buried on it."

Hurriedly, she read the description of the property, the landmarks and the measurements that would lead to the supposed treasure. Nowhere did her grandfather say what it was that was buried. "...My sister, your aunt, should have been the oldest son, for she is convinced of the legend's truth..." Elena skimmed the rest of the letter and stared at the trees beyond the balcony. That would have been her great aunt, someone she never knew. "...She has never forgiven me for not chasing after that imaginary treasure. She claims I robbed her of great wealth. But then, my sister always did have a greedy imagination..."

So neither her grandfather nor her father had gone looking for "the riches." She knew that her father was a cautious man, not at all adventurous. And from what he had said in this letter, her grandfather must have been the same. She read the letter through again. It seemed to her that good sense, not caution, must have stopped them. The whole thing sounded like something a child might have dreamed up. She, too, would think twice about searching for that treasure.

She got up and slid the papers once more under the clock. As she walked out onto the balcony, it hit her: knowing what was in the envelope had brought her no closer to her father. She hadn't known what to expect when she opened it, but she had to admit that her hopes had been high.

The April morning was clear and warm. Beyond the woods she could see a light mist clinging to the surface of the sea, and close by, in the trees, she heard a dove coo. Today, instead of soothing, the sound was melancholy—and unwelcome.

Her eyes wandered over the woods, searching for the spot where the sycamore and the fallen tree should be. David would be back soon. And, although the letter and the deed had turned out to be unimportant, when he returned she would show them to him and ask him what he thought.

During the rest of the day she looked for David, but it was late afternoon before he arrived. She was standing on a stepping stool, returning Ana's books to the library shelves, when she heard the front door open and close and his voice answering Mario's greeting. She heard the library door open and turned to see David, wearing a blue windbreaker and looking breeze-blown and fresh. He was carrying a bunch of white daisies. She put the last book in its place and stepped down from the stepping stool.

"Hi," he said, "it was a longer trip than I'd planned." He handed her the daisies. "These are for you."

"They're very pretty," she said, burying her face in the the flowers. "Thank you."

"Margaritas, aren't they?" he asked. When she nodded, he said, "Is Montalvo back?"

"No. Your mother said he'd return tonight."

She looked down at the flowers, wanting to tell him that she had seen Doctor Montalvo last night, but holding back, afraid of David's anger at his stepfather. "I opened the sealed envelope," she said instead, "the one I told you about. I don't think it's important. Would you like to look at it anyway?"

"Sure."

"I left it upstairs."

"I'll walk up with you."

They sat on the top step of the outside staircase. David read the letter and the deed, asking her to translate a word here, a phrase there.

"This is great, "he said, and read aloud. "... From the eastern base of that great red boulder, measure the length of four cornfields to the north and one to the east. The flat side of the great boulder will be completely exposed. You are standing on the spot where the treasure is buried..." He nodded seriously. "I'll bet these measurements are darned accurate." Then he read the letter again, silently.

Surprise, bewilderment, excitement—yes, she was sure it was excitement—all these expressions came and went on his face. She looked at him, disbelieving. He was falling for this nonsense! Finally, with a look she could not figure out, he asked, "Can I take these papers for a day or two?"

"Why?"

He looked up sharply. "I'd like to look them over."

"I can't let you have them, David. They're... they're sort of a trust. It's enough that I opened the envelope."

He handed her the papers. "I don't blame you for wanting to hang on to them," he said. But his words were edged with something like frustration. "I...I only wanted to study them a bit. There's something there that I can't quite figure out."

"I'm sorry," Elena said. "I'll think it over. Ask me again."

"Fair enough," David said, standing up. "Look, I have to see mother now. See you at dinner." At the bottom of the stairs, he turned. "Elena?"

She rose eagerly. "Yes?"

"I have to be on campus in the morning. Back on Thursday, though." He swung around and cut across the lawn toward the other wing.

As she watched David walk away, Elena thought, I should have let him take the papers. What difference would it make? He's only trying to help me. Yes, but why? I know I like him and he likes me, but is it more than that? Something in these papers caught his eye. I wish I knew what it was.

A short while later there was a knock at her door. She threw it open. "David," she said, and when she saw Sara, her face stung with color.

"You're getting pretty important around here, aren't you?" Sara said. "There is a telephone call for you. Over there." She pointed to the front end of the hall and then walked briskly toward the back stairs.

Elena ignored the sharp remark and ran to the phone. My father, she thought, it must be my father. She picked up the receiver. "*Listo*," she said breathlessly, and then, remembering where she was, "Hello!"

"It's about time." The voice was a woman's.

Elena swallowed back disappointment. "Who is this?"

"You know who it is. It's Luisa."

"No, I didn't."

"Yeah, well... Say, what did you tell my father that made him so mad? He was ready to wipe me out after you left."

"Nothing. Nothing more than you told me. If he's angry at you, that's not my fault. It has nothing to do with me."

"Maybe not your fault, but it does have to do with you. That's why I called. Because what I know about your father is more expensive now. Fifty bucks isn't enough. I want fifty more for the chewing out my old man gave me. So, it's one hundred dollars, Elena, and the longer you wait, the more it'll be."

"Luisa, are you deaf? Or merely stupid? I said no money. Why should I give you money—even if I had it? You've probably made up the whole story."

"You think I'm trying to con you? I could, I guess. You're dumb enough. Look, I already described him for you."

"Of course you described him. You saw him in the restaurant."

"Sure. But I saw him in the storeroom that night, too. And I'll tell you this much, he was having a hard time talking. Like he couldn't breathe."

"Now you're trying to scare me, Luisa. There are things that scare me, yes, but you're not one of them."

"Shit, if I wanted to scare you, I could. But all I'm doing here is feeding you the facts. That man was in real trouble. There was a lot of mumbling going on, then all of a sudden he called out, 'San Martín, help me!' And he sounded as if he really meant it."

Elena closed her eyes and tightened her hold on the telephone. That was her father! She remembered when he had dropped a large rock on his foot and broken a toe. In between other curses, he had called on San Martín to damn the rock as well as his own stupidity. San Martín, her father had said, was his "friend at court."

"Well?" Luisa's voice shot through the wire.

"All right, Luisa," Elena said, "I believe you. You've got to tell me, though. What was wrong with him? I have to know!"

"The money, remember?"

"Luisa, tell me! Is he all right?"

"Call me tomorrow. At the restaurant. After four-thirty. You should have the money by then." There was a loud click. Luisa had hung up.

CHAPTER FOURTEEN

A jumble of feelings went with Elena as she hurried back to her room. The feeling that finally burst into the open was anger. She was angry. At Luisa. A scalding anger that bubbled and hissed and threatened to boil over. What did that little witch think she was doing? Money! Money! One hundred *dollars*! She *does* know something about my father! And so does Juan Otero. He lied to me! Why? Why? He's as deceitful as his daughter! Twice I've asked him. Twice he's put me off.

Elena closed the bedroom door sharply. Through the open window came the sounds of Mario and Carlos at play at the edge of the woods: laughter, shouts, an argument. Her anger extended to Carlos. Stop fussing, Carlos, she muttered to herself. Stop being such a demanding little macho! She closed the window and her thoughts returned to the telephone call. My father *was* in that storeroom! And he's hurt. Fear cut into her angry feelings like a cold knife and she stiffened. But in a few seconds the inconsistency of anger won out. Luisa's lying, she told herself. Luisa's lying to get money. He's probably not hurt at all. And now all the crises of the last two weeks: the confrontation with her aunt, the decision to come to Los Angeles, the raw disappointment at Emerald Avenue, and Luisa's trickery all combined to trigger in Elena's mind a wave of childhood grievances against her father that were painful and not easily forced back into the depths from which they had surfaced. Yes, something was going on that she didn't understand. That was certain. But her father should have warned her somehow. He knew Carlos and she were coming. He should have let her know what was going on!

She was still struggling with the confusion of her feelings when, fifteen minutes later, someone knocked at her door. This time, surely, it would be David. She threw open the door and found Mrs. Addison standing in the hall.

"Miss Ana asked me to tell you that she and David will be dining at the home of friends," she said, smoothing the skirt of her gray striped dress. "Last minute arrangements, don't you know."

Elena stared blankly and nodded as the realization sank in. She wouldn't see David until Thursday. Four long empty days. If she had been thinking clearly, thinking at all for that matter, the darkness of her disappointment would have told her about herself and David. Mrs. Addison raised her voice, forcing Elena to hear her words.

"Left me with a lovely pork roast sizzling in the oven."

"That's too bad. Come in, Mrs. Addison."

The older woman sighed and tucked a wandering wisp of hair behind her ear as she walked into the room. "I always prepare a proper Sunday dinner. Well, I dare say, you and the boys will enjoy it. And Henry. Henry does love a juicy loin."

"I'm sure we will," Elena said, trying to smile.

Mrs. Addison eyed her for a moment and then said gently, "You look peaked. Are you all right?"

The unexpected concern from Mrs. Addison almost brought tears. "Yes, yes. It's only that I'm tired."

"Well, then, I'd best be tending to our dinner. I'll set the table in the breakfast room." She walked firmly to the door and started to open it, but instead, turned. "Something lying heavy on your mind, love? If you're wanting to talk, I can take time to listen."

"Thank you, Mrs. Addison. You're very kind. I'm fine. It's all this change to get used to."

"Nothing to be ashamed of. We all have trouble when things change. It's been nine years, and I still think of Miss Ana as Mrs. Martel, not Montalvo."

Elena looked across the room and caught her friendly gaze. What did Mrs. Addison know about last night? "Will Doctor Montalvo be here for dinner?" she asked.

"Him?" Mrs. Addison looked at her blankly. "He's not returned. If he had, Miss Ana wouldn't have gone off. He expects her to be as near as the next room, but *he* comes and goes where and when he chooses."

Now Elena was certain that nobody knew that Doctor Montalvo had come and gone again. Why?

Why would he do that? She said, "Ana told me he would be home tonight."

"And that's just when he'll be here. Late tonight." Mrs. Addison sniffed. "Him and that Jim Donald. Tight as thieves those two, with their special projects and special keys for that downstairs room."

"What are they doing there?"

"Only the walls know. But whatever it is, it's dusty work. That Jim Donald comes into my kitchen without wiping his feet and trails in all that powdery stuff." She stopped abruptly. "There. But I'm not one to gossip, and the applesauce will be burning. It may be just us, but I still intend to serve a tasty dinner." She nodded as, with firmness of purpose, she opened the door and closed it.

When the sound of Mrs. Addison's footsteps had faded, Elena slumped into the wing-backed chair. David hadn't cared about seeing her at dinner. So why had he brought her flowers? She reached out and touched the daisies on the table by her side. Whatever his reasons, she told herself, keep in mind that this isn't Camelot and you're not Guinevere. You're just a girl from the country who has yet to learn the city ways. She sighed. And if you had Merlin's magic, you'd spirit yourself back to Playa Blanca right now, wouldn't you?

Yes, it was true. She missed everything about Playa Blanca. Even her aunt, although they had parted unpleasantly. Tía Concha was not usually mean-spirited. It was only a fear of hunger that had made her so grasping in the last few months. Elena closed her eyes and imagined the table in the low-ceilinged kitchen where they had taken their meals. *Picadillo* and *carne asada* and *salsa fresca* and *frijoles. Frijoles*, refried, with long strings of white cheese melting on your chin and becoming an excuse for silly laughter. She missed the good-humored jibes of her cousins. She missed the narrow bed in the small room she shared with the three girls. But most of all she missed the barefoot walks on the beach with the sea breeze smelling of fish and shells and rocky islands, blowing her hair over her face. It was on one of those walks that she had met David, the boy who could speak only English and who claimed he could perform magic feats. Maybe he could. At that thought she shrugged, jumped out of the chair and called to Carlos that it was time to wash for dinner.

Perhaps it was Mrs. Addison's pork roast, which Elena forced herself to eat, or the memory of the stealthy footsteps of the previous night, or the thought that her father could be hurt and in pain, but her sleep was restless. During her waking moments, she took turns, it seemed, thinking of David and of Luisa. And all that thinking led her nowhere in regard to David, but, as to Luisa, sometime during the night she made up her mind.

In the morning, only Carlos and she were at the breakfast table. A breathless Mario came in to say that his father was home, that he was talking to him, and that he would meet Carlos out front in time for the bus.

Instead of answering Mario, Carlos sulked. "Where's *my* father, Elena?" he whined. "It is time we found him."

"Yes, Carlos," she said. "You're right. It is time that we found him."

Immediately after breakfast she knocked on Doctor Montalvo's study door.

"Enter." Doctor Montalvo was seated at his desk, his chair swiveled toward the hall.

"May I talk with you for a moment, señor?"

He nodded, indicating a chair. "Well, Elena, what can I do for you?" His face was grave but friendly.

Nonetheless, nervousness tightened her throat. How to start? Not at the beginning, because the beginning would make no sense to him. "Doctor Montalvo, I wonder if..." She stopped.

"You have a problem? Is that it?"

She nodded and, in a voice which she struggled to keep calm, said, "Is it possible to ask for one hundred dollars? I know that's a lot of money, but I need it to find my father. It will get me information."

"About your father?"

"Yes." She took a deep breath. "A girl I met at the restaurant told me she knew...well, there's no need to bother you with that. But since you were so kind about offering me money in advance, I thought maybe..."

"Of course, of course." He picked up the quartz paperweight on his desk. He seemed to be far away as he stared at it. Then with a quick, decisive motion, he returned it to the desktop. "This restaurant," he said. "It's close to where your father lived?"

"Very close. Carlos and I found it—no, that isn't how it was. We were taken to it by the police officers."

"Police?" he said sharply, leaning forward. And then, as if catching himself, he added more softly, "Now, now, Elena, you didn't tell me you were in trouble with the police."

"I'm not. It was they..."

"Ah," he said, his mouth tightening, his eyes alert, "you *went* to the police then. Why would you do that?"

What was he thinking? "No, Doctor Montalvo, we did not go to the police. They found us when we were lost, and because we were hungry, they drove us to that restaurant. They're friends of the owners."

"Ah-h, you were lost. I see." Slowly, he settled back in his chair. Again, he picked up the paperweight, turning it over and over in his hands. Finally he smiled and said, "Now, about the money. You can have it as part of your first week's pay. I assume you need it today?"

"If you can, señor. After my driving lesson, perhaps?"

"You can have it right now." He rose. "Let's hope the driving school doesn't disappoint you again. David isn't here to substitute."

So he had heard about that. She returned his amused look. "The instructor will be here," she said quietly. "I made sure of that."

"*Lo que será, será,*" he said. He reached into an inside pocket of his suit coat and brought out a tooled leather wallet. He placed two fifty-dollar bills on the desk before her.

"How can I thank you?" she said.

"There is no need to. I only hope this will help you find your father."

"I do, too," she said with a grateful little laugh. She had been dreading this meeting with him, and he had made it so easy. With the bills held tightly in her hand, she went out of the door.

Upstairs in her room she took her purse from the closet shelf and slipped the money into her wallet. She paused, frowning. Something was wrong. Her purse was too light. Even before she had spilled the contents of the purse onto the bed, she knew what it was. The packet of her father's letters was gone! Quickly, she searched the closet and Carlos' room and found nothing. Her gaze circled the sunny green and gold of her room, lingering on the vase of daisies on the mantle. Oh, no, the deed!

With hands that were wet and cold, she tilted the heavy base of the clock. The papers were right where she had put them, but there was something on the mantle that she had not put there. The daisies. They had been on the table by the wing-backed chair. She lowered the clock carefully and looked in the bathroom. There was no sign left of Carlos' untidiness, or hers, for that matter, and fresh towels were hanging on the rungs. Sara had been here. She had moved the flowers, but would she have dared to take the letters? Mrs. Addison would know.

Elena hurried across the gallery to the back stairs. The blue-tiled kitchen was empty, but someone was in the pantry. "Mrs. Addison, can we talk?"

Jim Donald, a loaf of bread in one hand, a butter dish in the other, stepped out of the pantry. A fine, gray dust covered his shoes and hair. He said, "Will I do?"

"No, thank you. It's Mrs. Addison I have to see. Or, better yet, Sara."

He grinned. "Sara's bumbling about somewhere. As for Mrs. Addison, you're out of luck like me." He put the butter dish on the counter. "Addie and old Henry are gone for the day, and I can't find the mustard. Know where she keeps it?"

She shook her head, and he shrugged and unwrapped the loaf of bread. "Have a sandwich with me?"

She wished she could say yes. With his fair hair flopping at each movement of his head, Jim Donald gave the impression of a long-legged, friendly puppy. Reluctantly, she shook her head. "I've just finished breakfast."

"Have another cup of coffee then."

"I can't. I have a driving lesson in..." She looked up at the clock. "...in three minutes."

"Out of luck again," Jim said. "No mustard, no company. My day just isn't going well."

Elena grinned. "Neither is mine," she said. "But I intend to change that."

CHAPTER FIFTEEN

Most of Elena's driving lesson was on freeways. And during that lesson, her problems were definitely forgotten. She thought of nothing but the car she was driving, her speed, the other cars and their speed, and, in between, her teacher's instructions.

When, at last, she brought the car to a stop on Gray Ridge Drive, she was not sure what was first in her mind: a sense of accomplishment or a desperate craving for a shower. Her clothes had felt damp and sticky ever since she had killed the motor on an on-ramp, and one by one a line of angry motorists had formed behind her car, a line that stretched all the way to the street below.

The instructor, a husky man named Petersen, sat placidly while she struggled to start the car. "No, it's not flooded," he reassured her in a cool, quiet voice. "You're just not used to all these buttons." But she had continued to have trouble, and the horns of the impatient motorists started blaring. Petersen stuck his head out the window and his voice had been neither cool nor quiet as he gave some unique instructions to the driver of the car behind them.

Now, as Elena climbed the stairs to her room, the sense of satisfaction from what Petersen had said was a job well done faded. All the worries of the night and morning sprang up on the staircase before her like hideous ghosts. But there was nothing she could do until four-thirty. Except see Sara, perhaps. And she had decided to let that go for a bit; the letters might still turn up. As for Luisa, the thought of the phone call to be made later that afternoon filled her with a mixture of anger and eagerness.

After lunch the eagerness began to fade. She was in the plant room with Ana answering correspondence when she recognized the shift in her feelings. She should not have to pay for information about her father. That was blackmail. She would have no part in it. No, she muttered to herself and looked up from the letter she was writing, afraid that she might have spoken aloud. Ana was looking out the window. If she noticed Elena's uneasiness, she said nothing about it.

By mid-afternoon, once Elena was alone and able to think more clearly, she had made a firm decision. She would not give in to Luisa's demands. No matter that she had borrowed the money from Doctor Montalvo. That was simple: she would return it. But the problem that remained was not simple: how to find out what Luisa knew.

At four-thirty she stood by the telephone in the upstairs hall, still without a plan. She stared out the window. Beyond the gates a soft afternoon breeze blew across the little meadow, and the yellow blossoms quivered. A bird, small and light as a wafted leaf, drifted over the meadow and then disappeared in the trees on the far side. All seemed at peace out there, while in here with her... She drew in a breath that was only a small part determination and reached for the phone. I'll sink or I'll swim, she told herself and hoped that inspiration would come and bail her out. She dialed the restaurant's number. The phone rang several times before it was answered.

"La Fonda." It was Luisa's voice.

"Hello, Luisa. This is Elena."

"Right on time. Did you get the money?"

"Actually, yes, but..."

"Well, how soon can you get down here?"

"No, Luisa, I'm not going..." Elena bit back the rest of her words. Go slowly, she told herself, you don't want to alienate her at this point. "Down to the restaurant? I can't."

"Sure you can. Where's the guy? He can bring you."

"He's not here. But that's not the point. I've been thinking it over. I'm not going to give you any money."

"Oh, yes, you are. Wait till you see what I've got."

"You're playing games again. Tell me now. What is it?" There was a long silence at the other end of the line, broken by the distant sounds of clattering dishes, voices and laughter. "Luisa," Elena said irritably, "is it something about my father?"

"Come and see."

"I can't. I have no way to get there."

"Oh, shit!"

The short, sharp words were a cry of frustration. Luisa was about to have a tantrum. Elena thought for a few moments. "Why don't you borrow your parents' car?" she said. "Maybe we could meet somewhere."

"I don't need you to tell me what to do," Luisa said sullenly. "I'd already figured that one out."

"That's good."

A sound like a hiss came over the wire before Elena heard Luisa's next words. "I'll be there in half an hour. You be waiting at the front door. Then you can show me around that fancy joint."

"No," Elena said quickly. "Absolutely not. It has to be somewhere else."

"Yeah? Where? In the middle of the road?"

"No, Luisa, not on the road. Let me think." Something tugged at her memory—perhaps the inspiration she had hoped for—and she said, "Remember the place we passed just below Gray Ridge Drive? The place called The China Cup?"

"Yeah, I remember it," Luisa said. "But it'll be crowded with people. No way."

"It closes at five. The people will be gone. I didn't mean inside, anyway. I noticed a bench near the back. We can sit there."

"If that's the best you can do, okay. But don't keep me waiting. And, Elena, don't forget the cash."

Elena put the phone down. She stood for a moment staring at a hunting scene on the wallpaper above the telephone table, wondering what she would do when she saw Luisa. Then, frowning, she went to Mario's bedroom door. Mario and Carlos were sprawled on the floor of the room, the television blaring.

"You two are supposed to be studying," she said.

Mario looked up and shrugged. Carlos rolled over on his back and nudged Mario. "Elena," he said in Spanish, "can you not see? That is what we are doing. I am learning English."

"Maybe *you* are," she answered him, "but Mario doesn't need to." Then in English she said to both of them, "Look, boys, be good and do your work. I have to be gone for about half an hour."

Carlos sat up. "Where are you going?"

"On an errand."

"Let me go with you."

"Not this time." From the door she called, "I won't be long."

Although a late sun was still shining, twilight gloom filled the woods as Elena hurried on the short-cut path toward the road. She paused at the sycamore and stared at the patterned sunlight in the open space. And what she saw in her imagination was David. David, sitting with her on the fallen tree trunk, looking with her at the Luisa thing, planning together how to get her to talk. But David wasn't here; she was on her own. A quick glance at the view of the coastline and she returned to the path, trudging firmly toward The China Cup.

As she neared the road, she heard the sound of a motor turning over and the screech of tires as it pulled away. A woman called something in a shrill voice. Then there was quiet. She climbed down the log steps, crossed the road, and waited for Luisa under the redwood sign. She was early, she knew, but as the minutes went by she began to wonder if Luisa would show up at all. Maybe Luisa had thought it over and come to the conclusion that Elena meant it, that she would give her no money. And without a pay off, Elena was sure that she would hear no more from Luisa.

She looked up eagerly each time she heard an automobile rounding the curve, only to slump back against the tree when a stranger's car went by. She was disappointed. To satisfy her ethical self she had told Luisa the truth about not giving her money. But underlying her words had been the not-too-ethical hope that Luisa would hear only what she wanted, that her arrogance and greed would win out. After all, Luisa held her only clues; she had to keep in touch with her.

Tires sounded on the asphalt again, and this time it was the Oteros' blue Mustang. It screeched to a halt at the side of the road, and Luisa, in a yellow sweat shirt with "Las Brujas" printed on it, got out of the driver's side. Elena straightened her shoulders, as if fortifying herself for the encounter, and walked toward her.

Luisa scanned the clearing around the building and said, "What a sleazy place."

"Hello, Luisa," Elena said pleasantly. She had to start out on the right foot; she had to make this meeting work.

It was clear that Luisa had no such thought. Manners, good or bad, were obviously not in her design. "What a sleazy place," she repeated.

Elena pointed to a bench near the back of the building. "We can sit there."

"It'll have to do," Luisa said. At the bench she turned her back and circled away from Elena. Then she whipped around, waving a white envelope in the air. "Do you know who wrote this?"

Elena shook her head. "No. How could I?"

"Guess."

"Stop playing games! Just let me see it."

Luisa moved closer, her arm extended. "Only a quick look—so you'll know."

Elena leaned forward. Luisa's long fingernails were bright red against the white of the envelope. It was addressed to Juan Otero. And the writing, the fancy capital "J" and the fancy "O," was her father's!

Luisa said, "Give me the money and I'll give you the letter."

"That letter isn't yours to give, much less sell. Besides, your father will tell me what it says."

Luisa grunted crudely. "My old man never saw this letter. I keep a lot of them. That's how I get even with him, watching him sweat out the letters that never come, watching him chase after the mailman and call the post office. He never figures I've got 'em."

"You're inhuman," Elena said. "What could he possibly have done to you to make you act that way?"

"That's my business." Luisa waved the letter and smiled. "And this one came in handy. I'll take the money now."

"What money? I said no money. I didn't bring any."

For one brief moment the smile remained on Luisa's lips, and then she snarled, "You bitch! You got me up here for nothing!" She hurtled toward Elena, the envelope still in her left hand, her right aimed at Elena's face.

Elena swerved, but Luisa's hand raked her cheek. She felt a hot, biting pain. She stepped back. "Stop it, you little fool!"

But Luisa pressed in, both hands flying. One hand hit hard over Elena's mouth, and she tasted blood. She swung her head away and kicked Luisa in the shinbone. With a curse, Luisa lunged forward. Elena was ready for her this time. She bent over and rammed her shoulder against Luisa's middle, then pulled back, dug her feet into the ground and shoved, sending Luisa sprawling. But with that shove she lost her balance and fell, too. Her hands felt the scraping burn of fine gravel as she hit the ground. She pushed herself up, waiting for another attack. None came. Luisa was still on the ground, stretching and reaching under the bench for a patch of white that lay under it. The letter!

Elena dove toward the bench and pulled at the envelope just as Luisa's fingers reached it. There was a tearing sound and Luisa was left with a small corner of the envelope. The rest was in Elena's hand. She grasped it tightly and started to crawl away. Luisa twisted herself upward and, with the leverage of the wooden bench at her back, grabbed Elena's hair and gave it a sharp pull. Elena's head yanked forward and she found herself half-kneeling, half-sprawling on the ground.

"Let go!" she yelled. Luisa pulled harder. Hot tears squeezed from Elena's eyes as she swung at Luisa's hands. Luisa hung on. Elena thrust herself forward and with all the strength she could muster jabbed her fist into Luisa's stomach.

Luisa pulled in her breath in a loud gasp, moaned, and doubled over.

With one great push Elena was up from the ground. She shot across the road, the envelope rolled tightly in her hand. As she scrambled up the log steps, she heard Luisa's angry calls and, in a few seconds, her footsteps on the asphalt. Elena's heart hammered as she ran into the woods. Luisa was a street fighter. She would claw her into shreds if she had a chance. Remembering, she brushed her cheek with the back of her hand. It was smeared with blood. She shuddered at the thought of Luisa's long fingernails. When she came to the place where the two paths met, she didn't hesitate. She took the one that led through the denser woods.

Birds hurtled noisily out of the pine branches, disappearing into the thick growth above. The sun had not yet set, but no light filtered through the trees. The dark shadows were filled with movement, but the only sound she heard was the sharp cracking of dry twigs beneath her feet. In a few minutes she was breathing hard. Panting, she stopped to listen, hoping that Luisa had given up. But Luisa had not. Her running footsteps sounded a short distance behind her.

Elena forced herself to keep moving. Hurry! Hurry! Her breathing was coming in short, painful bursts when she felt the ground give way beneath her left foot. She groaned and fell to her knees. Her ankle throbbed as she plunged into a tangle of scrub growth beside the path. The shrubs parted and then closed behind her. She flattened herself on the ground, willing her breathing to be still.

In a matter of seconds, a blurry spot of yellow came into sight. Elena buried her head. She heard the sound of Luisa's labored breathing directly above her, but Luisa didn't stop. Her footsteps pushed upward on the trail.

For a few minutes after Luisa went by, Elena did not move. Then she took a quick look around her. She could make out that behind her the ground dropped gently to a creek, then rose again. The highway, she figured, had to be beyond the far embankment. She rubbed her pulsing ankle and slid carefully down the incline. Every yard or so, she stopped to listen. She was halfway down when she heard the crackling of underbrush and footsteps once more on the trail. Cautiously, she edged her head around the trunk of a tree and saw a flash of yellow moving above her. Luisa was going back the way she had come, kicking up dirt and muttering as she pounded down the trail.

Elena closed her eyes and expelled her breath in grateful relief. She relaxed her fingers around the envelope. After a while, she got up. She stepped gingerly on her left foot. Her ankle was painful, but she could walk. Carefully, she waded through the creek and climbed the slope on the other side. Her guess had been right. She was standing above the highway, maybe half a mile away from The China Cup. There was a thicket of young trees on a little knoll near the edge of the asphalt. She huddled behind it to watch the road. A car or two went by and then, at last, she saw the blue Mustang. It was heading down the hill toward the ocean. She could go back now. As she rose, her hands started to tremble; her body, to quiver. The tension that had been holding her together was gone, leaving her limp and ragged. She pulled in a deep breath and let it out. Then she turned and started back toward the path.

CHAPTER SIXTEEN

It was almost night when Elena came to the end of the path. She was grateful for the concealing darkness. She wanted no one to see her until she had made repairs. Even though there was no one in sight by the pool or on the grassy slope of lawn beyond it, she circled the swimming pool by its outer rim, taking care to stay in the shadows of the oleanders. She had reached the outside staircase when she heard her name called.

"Elena, wait!" Carlos was running across the grass, Mario behind him. Carlos came to a standstill a few steps from her. "Someone has beaten up on you, Elena," he said, his eyes wide, his jaw jutting out belligerently. "Who was it?"

Elena shook her head. "No one beat up on me, Carlos. I turned my ankle and fell."

"Oh," Carlos said, and that short syllable was edged with disappointment. "But if someone *did* beat up on you, you would tell me, wouldn't you? I am your brother, and I would protect you."

"Yes, Carlos," she said, eager to be gone, "yes, yes."

But Mario, too, needed an answer. "You look awful," he said. "What happened?"

"I turned my ankle. I'm all right." She could feel the dried blood on her face and the tangles in her hair. Her feet, from her crossing of the creek, were mud-caked and soggy. She gave a quick, little laugh. "No matter how I look, I'm all right."

"You were gone a long time," Mario said.

"I know, but I'm here now... and everything's all right. I'll take a quick bath and then come downstairs." She hurried up the steps.

With the door to her room closed behind her, Elena unwound and sank slowly into the wing-backed chair. She stared with unseeing eyes at the dark rectangle of the window for a few moments and then, in a rush of returning awareness, sat up and switched on a lamp. She pulled the mud-stained envelope from her pocket.

She was disappointed; the corner of the envelope with the postmark was gone. She had last seen it in Luisa's hand. Quickly, Elena pulled out the letter inside and unfolded it.

"Amigo," it began. (So her father and Juan Otero *were* friends. Why had Señor Otero refused to tell her?) "My affairs," the letter went on, "are moving slowly, too slowly, and I am feeling great impatience. Particularly, since I dare not write to my children and let them know where I am. Under the circumstances, some of which you understand, I dare not. If María Elena, my daughter, arrives, Juan, it is safe now to tell her what you know, and, please, watch out for her." Elena looked at the date. Over two months ago. Her father *had* made arrangements for her to learn about him, but Luisa had interfered.

She went on reading. One sentence stood out. "Knowing you, Juan, I am sure that you have told no one, not even your good wife, what I am doing."

Strange. None of this sounded like her father. A vague feeling of distress filled her. All this secrecy. Why is it necessary? What does he need to hide? She sat staring at the letter, shaken and confused, until the dinner bell rang.

The bath *was* quick, but even so she was late. The soup had been served when she came into the dining room. As she seated herself, Doctor Montalvo looked sharply at her, his eyes narrowing.

Ana, too, looked pointedly at her and then spoke quickly. "Our Monday night suppers are light," she said, looking around as if for a subject of conversation. "It's Mrs. Addison's day off." Then she added, "Tell me, Elena, is there any word of your father?"

"Sara says that..." Carlos caught himself, his hand over his mouth.

Elena threw him a wondering glance. To Ana, she said, "I hope to have some news soon."

The rest of the meal was eaten in an uncomfortable silence. She felt her face grow hot as Doctor Montalvo looked at the scratches on her cheek. He said nothing, but his glance kept returning to her face.

Sara served supper, and Elena was reminded of the missing letters. But that seemed long ago—and unimportant. The letter that mattered now was the one she had wrested from Luisa and which she had to return to Juan Otero. Maybe she could do that tomorrow. Tonight, a telephone call telling him about that letter would have to do.

After supper she settled Carlos and Mario with their books and went to the telephone in the hall. She dialed the number of La Fonda. When a woman answered, she said, "May I speak to Señor Otero, please. This is María Elena Vargas."

The woman grunted something unclear and left the phone. Elena waited for what seemed a long time, listening to the commotion of voices, music, and the sounds of the cash register that reached her through the line. Finally, when she was beginning to believe that she had been forgotten, she heard Señor Otero's pleasant voice.

"Señorita Vargas, I apologize for keeping you waiting." There was a sharp click and the background noises disappeared. "Ah-h, now we can talk. We are alone."

"Señor," she said, "I called because I know now that you are my father's friend, that you were in his confidence. I also know that he asked you not to talk to anyone, not even to me, about his affairs until he told you it was all right to do so."

There was a long silence during which she could hear Juan Otero's breathing. Softly, in and out. He had been stopped short, she was sure. At last, he said, "Yes, it is true. I only wonder how you know. He, in turn, promised that I would hear from him. I have not."

But he did write! The words were shouted only in her mind. She was not sure yet how to tell him about Luisa or the letter. "Look, señor," she said, "tell me now. When did you last see him?"

She heard him sigh. "Yes, I will tell you. What difference can it make? I saw him last in January."

"How was he?"

"Troubled. Yes, troubled. But other than that, I would say he was all right. Yes, he was all right when he left me."

"Where did he go?"

No answer.

"When you *did* see him, did he talk about me, señor?"

"I am not at all sure I should say this, but, yes, he was worried about you. About your safety. He was worried about a man who might try to contact you."

"Contact me? For what?"

"He didn't say. Or if he did, I must apologize, I have forgotten."

"It doesn't matter," she said quickly. "No one's tried to contact me about anything." Except for Luisa, she thought, and stared thoughtfully out the window to the open spot in the darkness that was the little meadow. Juan Otero had been honest with her. She had to be honest with him. "Señor," she said, "I've just found out that my father did write to you."

"What?"

"He wrote you in February."

"I received no such letter."

"I know. Luisa had it."

"Luisa?" he said in a cold flat voice. "Luisa? Are you sure?"

"Yes, I'm sure. She brought the letter up here a few hours ago. I have it now."

"You have the letter? What is this? What is going on?"

She should have waited. It was too hard to explain over the telephone. But there was no time now for regrets. She had provoked the question and Juan Otero was expecting a reply. "Señor," she said rather breathlessly, "I don't like to say this, but Luisa took the letter my father wrote to you and hid it. And when she learned I was his daughter, she tried to sell it to me."

"Sell it? I do not understand."

"She wanted money. One-hundred dollars."

"What!"

"One-hundred dollars. A lot of pesos, señor. But even if I'd had the money, I wasn't going to buy it. The letter is yours."

"I see. And *you* have the letter now. No, I certainly do not understand. But if what you say is true, I do not like what I am hearing."

"I am… I am sorry, " she said feebly. "I'll try to bring the letter to you tomorrow."

"Thank you, yes." And then, "No, I do not like it at all," Juan Otero said.

Her mouth was dry as she asked, "Do you think Luisa might have other letters that my father wrote to you?"

"If she does," came the curt reply, "I will see that they are returned to me." A pause. "I also made another promise to your father, and that was to help you if I could. Are you comfortable in your friends' home? Is there anything I can do?" His words were courteous, but stiff and cold.

Had she ever been more miserable? She stared at the wallpaper, blinking hard as the hunting scene blurred. What could she say? "Thank you. The Montalvos are very kind to me and Carlos."

"There is nothing I can do for you?"

"No, thank you."

"Well, I will see you tomorrow then."

She said goodbye and walked slowly to her room. Had she been unkind? Maybe she could have told him about Luisa at some other time. And if she had waited, what then? Telling a man that his daughter is a cheat isn't going to get more palatable by putting that telling on to steep like tea. Well, it's done, she told herself, and it's the truth, and... All right! So I'm not a diplomat. She opened the bedroom door and went in.

The lamp was on. One of the French doors was open and the sheer curtains, undrawn, stirred in an ocean breeze. There was no hesitation in her movements. She walked directly to the clock on the mantle. She needed to read the letter to Juan Otero once more. But with her hand on the base of the clock, she stopped. There had been a sound. It whispered from behind her, no more loudly than the breeze filtering through the silk curtains. A rustling sound, muffled by the door of the closet. She turned around, tiptoed to the door and pressed her ear to the wood paneling.

"Carlos?"

No response.

"Carlos? Are you in there?"

A choked little whisper answered her. She opened the door. Carlos was crouched in a tight huddle against the back wall. "Elena," he whimpered, "please don't be mad at me."

"Mad? Why should I be?" She dropped to the floor beside him. "Are you all right? What are you doing in here?" And then she saw the bundled letters that had disappeared from her purse that morning lying next to him. They were tied clumsily with new twine. "My letters. What are you doing with them?"

"Putting them back. I borrowed them for a little while."

"You what? Why?"

"To show Sara. She wanted to see them."

"Sara?" Elena's voice rose to a high pitch. "Sara?"

"Don't be angry. Please."

"Angry?" she said, and all of the day's frustrations burst from her. "Oh, yes, I am angry. The saints know it, so you had better know it, too! I do not like it at all that..." She stopped abruptly. Señor Otero had just said those words to her about a missing letter. She shook her head and breathed deeply. Then she stood up and held her hand out to Carlos. "Come on, we don't need to stay in here."

He followed her into the room and sat at the foot of the bed. She sat in the chair facing him. "You could have asked me for the letters, you know."

He stared at the floor. "Sara told me not to. Not till we found out where Papá was. She was sure you knew and wouldn't tell me."

"What business is it of hers?"

Carlos looked up and she saw that his eyes were filling. "Sara is my friend," he said stiffly. "She wants to help me. She said I had a right to know where Papá was and that you could find him if you really wanted to." He ran the back of his arm across his eyes. "Elena, where is Papá? Sara said his letters would be sure to tell, but they didn't."

She leaned forward, frowning. "I don't know where he is. What made you think I did?"

He stared at her, a forlorn, confused Carlos with a lone tear rolling along the side of his nose. He shrugged.

It was the shrug that did it. She jumped up and sat beside him. She had her arms around him, her face against a tear-wet cheek. She had been so concerned with her own feelings that she had forgotten to think of him. "I would never lie to you about something so important," she said gently, and he buried his dark head in her shoulder. "I want to find him as much as you do."

She hugged him tighter. "No matter what, Carlos, remember, we have each other." But she sensed that he wasn't comforted—and that was understandable. Neither was she.

CHAPTER SEVENTEEN

It was only five days until the fiesta, and the piñata that Elena had agreed to make was barely started. Henry Addison, with only a small grumble, had made room on a work table for her. On that first day he had moved to the other end of the room and opened up a tool chest, but he did nothing with it. Instead, he watched her struggle to build a light wire frame for the clay pot that would hold the favors. There had been a couple of unbelieving snorts before he walked over and said, "Here, let me do that."

When it came to deciding the shape of the piñata, there had been another obstacle for Elena to overcome. Carlos wanted it to be made in the shape of a bull, Mario, a lamb. "A lamb it will be," Elena said, giving Carlos a pointed look, "for many reasons." She had not shared the fact that the most compelling reason was that to make a bull, as far as she was concerned, was impossible and that, with some luck, they might come up with a recognizable lamb.

The morning after her talk with Juan Otero, she spent the hour after breakfast in the workroom, cutting up newspapers and mixing glue for the papier-mâché cover that would go on the piñata's wire frame. Then, because there was something she wanted to resolve as quickly as possible, she went to see Ana.

The door of the plant room was slightly open and the air smelled of newly wet soil. Ana was watering a basket of grape ivy, a pensive look on her face.

"Ana?" Softly. She didn't want to take her by surprise.

"Why, Elena, come in." Ana placed the watering can on the hearth and returned to the basket of ivy. "Isn't this lovely? The leaves arc so green and glossy—I don't need a glass to see that. And look at that ficus. Did you ever see anything growing so tall? There are so many lovely things to see in the world. It's a shame we must look at anything else...anything sordid, unpleasant." Ana stretched her arms out wide above her shoulders. "Well, dear Elena, today I, for one, refuse to look at anything but a beautiful world." And then she added, "But aren't you early?"

"Yes. I wanted to talk with you."

Ana sank into her favorite wicker chair. "I'm glad you're here. No matter how I try to persuade myself, things seem gloomy today. I don't like being alone with my thoughts."

Maybe it was the lonely hours that Elena had spent with only gloomy thoughts for company that persuaded her to read between the lines. "Would you like me to stay with you this morning?" she asked.

"But you have a driving lesson."

"I can skip that, can't I?"

"Would you?"

"Of course."

"Elena, you're a dear." Ana sighed and turned to look out the window.

Elena bit back her disappointment. It was the driving lesson she had come to talk about. She had wanted to take more time than yesterday. She had wanted to see Juan Otero. When Ana sighed again, she said, "Has something happened? Is something wrong?"

"Nothing," Ana said without turning. And then, swinging around, "Oh, Elena, that's not true." Her voice was low and breathless. "Something *is* wrong, and I'm afraid…afraid of finding out what it is." A pause. "No matter what David thinks, I'm sure you have nothing to do with this."

David. Elena's face grew warm. She moved restlessly. If her cheeks were going to glow and her heart was going to race in this ridiculous way at every mention of his name…

Ana stared once more out the window. Her face was tense and still. Only her fingers moved, tapping the chair arm soundlessly. In a little while, she started to say something and stopped. Finally, she looked at Elena. "But it was you who came to talk. What is it? What's on your mind?"

Elena stood up. "Nothing important, really. Besides, I'd better go call the driving school to cancel. I'll be right back."

Halfway up the stairs she stopped. Ana had said something after she had mentioned David's name. "I'm sure you have nothing to do with this," was what Ana had said. This? This? *I* have nothing to do with *this*? Whatever this was, it was something that Ana did not want to look at. She had said so. Ana's eyes! Was that why she could see better at some times than others? In one of Sylvia Lewis' books on psychology she had read that the mind could do strange things, like cause false pregnancies and even some kinds of blindness. Maybe something like that was happening to Ana. Today Ana was very worried about *this*—whatever it was—and her eyes were worse. Well, David would have the answer. He was the one who had blurted out, "Where do you fit in?" Thursday would soon be here. As for now, she had two telephone calls to make. She rushed up the rest of the stairs.

After calling the driving school, she dialed La Fonda. "This is Elena," she said to Juan Otero. "I'm sorry, but I can't bring your letter today."

"No matter, señorita. *Lo que será, será.* But I have something to tell you." She heard him draw in a long breath and exhale it. "I have talked with Luisa...at length. Late last night she remembered that she did, indeed, have another of your father's letters." He gave a quick, sharp laugh. "Needless to say, I have that letter now."

Elena was silent for a moment, not sure of what to say. Finally, she asked, "What did he say? Where is he?"

"The news is old. When he wrote the letter in the middle of March, he was in the desert near Villa Rey in Tamaulipas."

Tamaulipas! He'd gone to search for that treasure after all. But why not tell her? Why the secrecy? There must be more to it. "What did he say?" she repeated.

There was something suspiciously like a grunt at the other end of the line, and Juan Otero said, "Only that he was well, that I was to keep his whereabouts unknown, and that I was to watch over you. But, remember, that was in March."

"Yes," Elena said. "Over a month ago. Do you think something's wrong?"

"No, no. In any case, there is no need to worry. Your father told me that his business had to be completed by May 15, and it is already the end of April. Let us be patient."

A little laugh escaped her. "That's not easy to do."

"No, it is not, is it? But let us do our best. Remember, we may hear from him again soon."

He was trying to be comforting, she realized that, but she was sure that he was worried, too. Still, better a little than nothing at all. At least, she knew where her father had been in March and something of what he was doing.

At the other end of the line she heard Juan Otero clear his throat. "Señorita Elena, I want to apologize for my daughter..."

"No, please," she interrupted. "It's not your fault."

"Well, we will leave it at that. Now, remember, if you need us, Carmen and I are here."

There was no coldness in Juan Otero's words today. The doubts that had arisen when she had told him about Luisa had obviously been resolved. Today she sensed a genuine warmth in his offer of help. She thanked him and hung up.

Going down the stairs, she felt better than she had in days. She spent the morning trying to make Ana feel better, too. She told her of the boys' games and their silly arguments. She told her about the piñata and the crooked leg Mario had made for their lamb. By the time Ana was ready to leave at noon, she was in better spirits.

"See what you have done for me," she said. "I am going to lunch with friends. I should be back by three." At the door she turned. "Relax this afternoon, Elena. We've done all the work we need to do today. Come on, come on, return those papers to the drawer. We'll leave together."

Before she went upstairs, Elena stopped in the library. She found a worn copy of *Gone With The Wind* and took it to her room to read. But, over and over, her mind left the printed pages. Finally, she put the book down and wandered out to the balcony.

How my life has changed, she thought. Last year at this time, she thought with a sigh, I was in a place I called home. She closed her eyes, longing to hear the sounds of Playa Blanca: the unusually sweet chimes of Abelardo's pushcart as he rolled it on the uneven dirt streets selling ices, the church bells that clanged dissonantly at noon, the clucking of old Pancho's hens next door. She longed even for the sound of the arrogant rooster that crowed almost daily during the hours of siesta.

Last year at this time I had just refused to marry Alejandro. I was so sure of myself. I had a job (no matter that I earned so little) and a home, and a father who would always be there if I needed him.

From the eaves above her came a rustling sound, and a pigeon shot from the roof to the space above the treetops, riding the currents of air like a surfer, at last disappearing into the woods.

Elena bit her lip. She had had real security, a security she had held too lightly. And now, like a child's bright balloon, that security had slipped away, lost, irretrievable. She sighed and drew in a breath that was nine-tenths exasperation. *Basta*, she told herself, enough! She pressed against the balcony railing, glanced up at the sky and down again.

Below her the water of the swimming pool glinted with sparks of sunlight. She had never been in a swimming pool. Oh, she could swim, and well. What child in Playa Blanca could not? So, if she had nothing to do but wait—for her father, for David, for the boys and Ana to return—and alone at that, by all the saints, she would make the best of it. Back in her room she quickly put on one of the bathing suits Ana had given her. She slipped on a loose-fitting dress over it and, carrying a large bath towel, went down the outside staircase to the pool.

She swam a few lengths and then floated on her back, counting the wisps of clouds that drifted like straying sheep in the sky. After a while she dived under water. Her hair clung to her face as she surfaced. She grabbed the rounded edge of the pool, brushed her hair away, and found herself looking at a pair of bare feet. Her gaze went from the feet to dust-covered jeans, to a discolored tee shirt and to a blond beard that almost hid a grin. Jim Donald.

"I've been watching you swim," he said. "You're pretty good." He extended his hand and when she took it he pulled her up on the deck beside him. "Want me to get you a towel?"

"No, thank you." She pointed to the blue-roofed pool house. "My towel is in there." She ran inside to dry off and when she returned she was wearing the dress over her damp bikini.

Jim was seated at one of the patio tables, a plate with a sandwich and salad in front of him. He took a bite of the sandwich and looked up. "You've gone and done it," he said. "Covered up that great bathing suit." She blushed at his remark, and he grinned. "Addie fixed me lunch. Want some?"

"No, thank you. I've had my lunch."

Jim put the sandwich down and patted a chair. "Keep me company, won't you?"

Why not? she thought, and sat across from him. Except for Mrs. Addison, Jim Donald is the only person I've met in Los Angeles who makes me really comfortable. Besides, I'd like to know more about what he does in that locked room.

They sat silently for a while and then she smiled at him and said, "How is your work as 'assistant of sorts' to Doctor Montalvo going?"

He kept chewing as he shrugged.

"That's not much of an answer," she said. "What do you do there? Or is it a deep, dark mystery?"

"It's not a mystery, even if it is big stuff."

"Good," she said, and her chin motioned toward the playroom door. "Then you can show me what's in there."

"Can't do. I have my orders. Nobody goes in there."

Elena shrugged. "Certainly sounds like a mystery to me. Sounds like that room's going to be locked up forever."

"No way. We'll be done by May fifteenth."

Elena stiffened, Señor Otero's words echoing in her mind. Even in the bright sunlight, she felt a chill slide down her spine. She struggled to keep her voice casual as she said, "That's a long time to keep a secret. What're you doing in there?"

"You wouldn't be interested."

"Who says? I'm interested in everything."

"Villa Rey, too? Bet you've never even heard of it."

"Villa Rey? You mean it has something to do with Villa Rey?"

Jim's face and neck reddened. "I'm not going to talk anymore," he said, and picked up his sandwich.

She watched him take a big bite and then she turned to stare at a yellow hibiscus on a shrub beside him. She wasn't going to learn any more from him. Not now. But something was going on that she didn't understand. And the something had to do with Villa Rey in Tamaulipas where her father had been. But what possible tie could there be between the Montalvos and her father? The answer, she'd bet, was behind the locked door in the playroom. She had to get in there. Abruptly, dark blue denim covered the yellow hibiscus, and she looked up to find Jim Donald standing by his chair, his plate in hand.

"Be right back," he said. "Time for dessert."

She stared at him as he walked into the kitchen, but she was really seeing three other people: Ana, who was deeply troubled today, maybe about her; David, who had urged her to look at all her papers, who had wanted to borrow the deed to her father's land; and Doctor Montalvo, who had something to do with Villa Rey.

Jim returned, eating a great wedge of apple pie.

She smiled at him across the table and said, "Whatever you do behind that door, I know one thing. It makes you dusty."

"Sometimes," he said, wolfing down the rest of the pie. He wiped his mouth on the back of his hand

and stood up. “Gotta go now. Gotta get back to work.”

She watched him pad across the lawn to the playroom. He had told her more than he should have, she was sure, but that telling hadn’t provided answers, only questions. The person she needed to talk with was not Jim Donald. It was David.

CHAPTER EIGHTEEN

Just before Jim Donald went into the playroom, he turned and waved to Elena. And as she smiled and waved back, a movement in the window above Jim's head caught her eye. Someone was watching her from the plant room, someone taller than Ana. Doctor Montalvo? More likely Henry Addison, she told herself, and turned away.

She remained in the chair by the pool for another few minutes. The broken pieces of information that she had gathered were arranging and rearranging themselves in her mind like the fragments in a kaleidoscope. None of the results satisfied her. So she gave it up as a tiresome exercise and plunged into the pool.

The swim and a shower refreshed her...somewhat. Her mind would not shake loose its muddled thoughts. Only one conclusion stood out clearly. She had to get a look into the playroom. But how? That was the question that occupied her as she went down the stairs to report to Ana. She knocked lightly. "Ana, may I come in?"

The door swung open and David was there. "Come in, of course. I'm waiting to see mother."

Maybe it was the shock of seeing him, or maybe it was the chill that edged his words, but something took the gladness away from her. "David," she said dully, "you're back. And this isn't even Thursday."

"No, it's not Thursday." He turned to the window. "What were you doing down there?" His chin jutted toward the pool.

So his was the face at the window. "Why, swimming. Your mother was gone, and I..."

"You don't have to account for your time to me," he said. "You don't work for me."

For a moment she was at a loss for words, but only for a moment. "If you don't want answers," she said crisply, coming alive again, "please don't ask me questions."

"I asked what you were doing with Jim Donald."

"No, you didn't."

"Well, I meant to. What were you doing?"

"Talking," she said.

"Talking," he repeated in a flat tone. "What about?" She opened her mouth to answer, but he spoke again. "Sorry. I have no right to ask that. It's clear anyway that it was a personal conversation."

David was jealous! Wasn't that wonderful? "David," she said, trying not to smile, "listen to me. How personal can questions about that locked door in the playroom be?"

David stood for a moment looking down at her. There was something in his eyes, something behind the dark angry look that made her wonder what he was thinking. His shoulders sagged. "The playroom. So you know about that. Listen, Elena, I'm sorry.

I'm damn well steamed about something, but I don't have to take it out on you."

"That's exactly what I think. But since you say you're sorry... And about that locked room. I asked him to show it to me, but he said no, absolutely no. Will you?"

"I wish I could. I haven't been able to get in there myself." He put his hand under her chin and tilted her head to one side. "That's an ugly scratch. How did you get it?"

"In a fight with Luisa." She grinned. "But how do you say it here? You want to see the other guy?"

"That's almost right."

He had not moved away. His hand was still holding her chin lightly. Confused, she said quickly, "Let me tell you how Luisa and I..." But she stopped to sense the nearness of his face, to wonder if he was smiling softly, as she was. What could she do about the warmth that was rushing to her cheeks, about the pounding heart that was so loud it was embarrassing? And then she knew. "Kiss me, David," she said, and there was a fleeting grin on his face as his mouth closed over hers.

In a moment he raised his head. He started to say something, but before he could speak there came a sound from the hall. He squeezed her arm and spun around.

"Mother," he said, "you're back at last. I've been here for an hour."

Ana walked into the room. "I know I'm late," she said. "Someone else was driving, of course, and I couldn't get away."

It was impossible to tell if Ana had seen the kiss. Her green eyes looked at them pleasantly enough, and she was smiling as she said kindly, "Elena, I have some things to talk over with David. If you don't mind, dear... You can have the rest of the afternoon to yourself."

Elena murmured, thank you, and somehow got herself out of the room. She circled the entry hall and went up the stairs, wondering at her feelings. She wanted to dance, she didn't want to dance. She wanted to sing; she was afraid to. She wanted to talk to somebody; no, no, she did not. What she wanted was to be with David. That was all.

In her room Elena curled up in the wing-backed chair, glad to be alone. Carlos' schoolbooks were scattered on the table beside her and *Gone With The Wind* lay open on the floor where she had left it earlier. She picked it up and put it on the table. Ashley...Rhett... She smiled. Scarlett could have them. She had David.

No sooner did the smile come, then it went. David's kisses had thrust her problems into the background—but just for the moment. Her worries were back, the bits and pieces blowing about in her mind as in a windstorm. If only there had been more time to talk to David.

At five o'clock Carlos had not shown up and she began to wonder where he was. She went down to the kitchen to look for him.

"Indeed, they were here," Mrs. Addison said. "Hungry as bears in spring, don't you know. Put away more than half of the cookies I baked this morning." She was at the stove, stirring a rich, brown gravy. The kitchen smelled of beef and spices.

"Do you know where they are now?" Elena asked.

Mrs. Addison raised her head. "They were talking in that half-English, half-Spanish they use now about going to their special hiding place."

"The woods? I'll never find them."

"It's not Mario's place in the woods those two were talking about, I know that. Still, it would take old Sherlock Holmes himself to figure out what they meant." She put the wooden spoon on the counter and turned. "'A watched pot never boils,' Elena. Leave them alone, and they'll come home."

Elena thanked her and headed back across the grass to the staircase. She was halfway there, wondering where to look next, when she heard footsteps and soft giggles. She swung around.

Carlos and Mario stood a few paces behind her, their hands, their faces, their jeans, and even a strand of Mario's hair brushed with a fine gray dust. There they were, as if dropped from the sky. And last night, when she was returning from meeting Luisa, they had appeared in the same way. "Where did you two come from?" she asked.

Mario said, "We want to show you something real neat." He gave a quick glance toward the playroom.

"You two have schoolwork to do now. Show me after supper."

Mario said, "Uh-uh. It's gotta be right now." He gave her a daring little grin.

She thought, why he looks like Carlos! With those smudged-up faces, those two are like a pair of circus clowns. She followed his look to the bed of blue lilies and the bushes that grew along the outside wall of the playroom. Three of the lilies were lying bent to the ground. Directly behind those lilies, she thought, are the windows of the locked room, and that's where the boys came from. They had figured a way to get in! Could she? *Should* she? Better not to ask. She knew what she was going to do. "Mario," she said, "have you been in the locked room?"

Mario looked at his feet and nodded.

"And how did you get in? The window?"

Mario shot her a quick look, returned his gaze to his feet, and nodded once more.

"Hasn't your father asked you to stay out of there?"

Mario's head jolted upwards. "Are you going to tell him?"

"Not now. I have to think about it. As for you, Carlos, what did I tell *you*? Don't make trouble, I said, and going into that place means trouble. Do you hear?"

"Am I deaf?" Carlos shot back. "Anyway, there's nothing in there but old stuff. Junk, huh, Mario?"

"I don't know," Mario said somberly. "It's my father's…"

"Junk!" Carlos said loudly. He swaggered toward the staircase and then thought better of it. "You have the cat's look, Elena," he said, turning. "You are planning something. Is that not so?"

Carlos' words set her back for an instant, but they shouldn't have. In Playa Blanca he had been a constant source of irritation to her and to her friends, popping up wherever she was, no matter how guarded her plans had been. "Don't try to know everything, Carlos," she said. "Go on upstairs."

For one long minute after the boys left she stared at the shrubbery. Then, before her determination could crumble, she hurried to the workroom. There she picked up a small hammer, a screwdriver, and a flashlight and rolled them in a length of paper toweling. She shoved them under her sweater and returned to the spot with the broken lilies.

Glancing over her shoulder at both wings of the house, she stepped over the blue flowers and dropped to her knees. Carefully, she lifted and pushed the low-hanging boughs of a mock orange bush. A branch snapped with a loud crack that made her heart jump crazily, but no one came running at the sound. She shoved the roll of tools ahead of her. Lying flat on her stomach, she squirmed and pushed halfway under the shrub. Only a few more inches to go and she would be by the window. But even as she thought that, she heard something that made her freeze. Footsteps moved on the cement walk that bordered the U between the wings. And her feet were still out there like a pair of beacon lights, making sure she could be seen!

Dear Mary...Teresa...any of you sweet sainted people who are not too busy to hear me, please, please, *please*, let the lilies hide my stupid feet! The seconds seemed like years as the footsteps came closer, reached the flower bed, and continued past it. Her prayer had been answered. Cautiously, she raised her head. Over the clumps of lilies she watched Jim Donald open the playroom door. And that meant that she had just run out of luck. Because now it was too late to get into the locked room.

Well, I'm here, she told herself, so I might as well take a look in the window. She pulled herself the rest of the way under the shrub. There was more headroom now. The boys had obviously cut away some branches, and she was able to kneel. Slowly, very slowly, pressing her hand against the side of the house for support, she turned awkwardly to face the window. She raised her head to the level of the sill and looked over it.

Although there was a narrow gap between the drawn drapes, she saw nothing. The room was dark. She pressed her face to the glass and squinted, trying to accustom her eyes to the darkness. It was at that moment that she heard the sound of a key and the snap of a bolt. The door to the locked room squeaked just before an inch-wide strip of light split the heavy curtains. Elena jerked her head away from the glass. She remained very still for an instant, and then, once again, brought her face close to the window. Now she could see a work table covered with muslin. On it was chiseled sand-colored rock. Jim, whistling almost soundlessly, dragged a wooden stool into her view and then, out. The stool creaked with his weight; she thought, he must be sitting on it. She could hear his movements clearly. If only she could see what he was doing. She moved her head, angling it a bit, hoping to see more, but she could not. What she did see was a wedge-shaped hole in the lower pane of glass. This must be why she could hear so well. It was also why the boys could get into the room. What problem for a little hand to reach the window lock? None. And hers? Maybe, but, in any case, she would have to wait until another time. For now, she could only listen to what was going on.

With that thought she stiffened, her fingers tightening on the sill. If she could hear Jim, could he hear her, too? Of course. What would happen if she snapped another twig? Her knees were jammed into a rough bed of sticks and gravel, and they hurt. But she dared not move. That was the thing. She was trapped there until he decided to leave. She heard the stool creak again, and then two or three unhurried steps toward the window. He *has* heard me! She was rigid as Jim's hand came around the side edge of the curtain. What would she say? What could she say? But Jim was not drawing wide the drapes. Instead, he was pulling them together. Her shoulders slackened and one by one she loosened her fingers and pulled them away from the sill. She leaned her head against the wall of the house. She had done this to herself. Somehow, she would have to wait it out.

In a moment she heard the metallic sound of a bolt and the opening of a door. Jim is leaving, she thought. But almost immediately, she knew that she was wrong. Someone had come in.

"Well, Jim," she heard Doctor Montalvo say, "how is our Huastec beauty coming? Is she in the shape Pablo hoped for?"

"Sure looks that way."

A few heavy strides that were not Jim's. There was a series of light taps and scrapes and Jim's tuneless whistle. A loud clang as a metal object fell to the floor, and then Doctor Montalvo spoke again.

"By God, that's a find. Look there, isn't that paint on her arms?"

"Sure is, professor. Decorations, like the book says."

A long period followed during which she heard only shuffling footsteps and sanding sounds.

"How's the temperature?" Doctor Montalvo asked. "You are watching it closely?"

"Sure. I check it all the time."

Doctor Montalvo said, "We have a treasure here. Probably three of the best examples of Huastec art of the Classic period. I would say close to 500 A.D." His voice rose. "Look at the pale pink stone. Almost flesh-colored. Huastec, definitely. No matter that they were found so far north."

"Boy, you sure never know, professor. Those Indians must've really got around. Worth a lot of green, I'll bet."

Doctor Montalvo gave a short hard laugh. "We would be talking about millions if we had another year at Villa Rey. That damn fool will ruin everything if we don't find him soon."

Villa Rey again! Elena drew in her breath. And millions of green? Of course, they meant money.

"Why the hurry?" Jim asked.

"Legalities," Doctor Montalvo said. "There is a hundred-year ownership clause that expires on May fifteenth."

"Then what? Does the government take it?"

"Not in this case. This is a family matter." Doctor Montalvo sounded sullen. "The clause was introduced by an old eccentric who wanted to see his desert transformed into a garden. If after one hundred years, none of his descendants have developed the land, it is to go to the Convent of the Little Sisters in Tampico. And that convent is still in existence."

Jim gave a sharp, little whistle.

"The nuns do not worry me," Doctor Montalvo said. "I have an arrangement with them. What worries me is that stupid man. But I have a plan to flush him out. I do not intend to lose my treasures. They belong to me. I uncovered them."

A long pause, then she heard Doctor Montalvo clear his throat. "All right, Jim, lock up now. Something's come in that we need to look at."

Elena stayed motionless as the door was bolted and the two men came outside and walked toward the garages. The room was empty, waiting for her, but she was no longer in a hurry to see it. It was her own room that she had to get to now. The deed. She had to look at it. Could that land in Tamaulipas be the same land that Doctor Montalvo was talking about? He had called the things in the locked room treasures. But then he had claimed they were his. Why? What was this all about? Who was Doctor Montalvo anyway?

CHAPTER NINETEEN

Elena pushed the tools under a low-hanging branch and shook her head. What had she intended to do with them? She backed out slowly from beneath the shrubs. Halfway out, she paused. Better take a look, she thought. I'll have a hard time explaining myself if someone sees me. She scanned the lawn and pool area. Good. There's no one there.

But as she clambered out of the shrubbery and climbed over the lily bed, she found that someone *was* watching her. David was on the balcony by the outside staircase, waving.

The wave she returned him was less than half-hearted. She had wanted to look as pretty as she felt for David, and she was a mess! Her shirt and pants were not only mud-stained, they were wrinkled and stuck with bristles and dry leaves. And her hair. That was the trouble with having it long. It swept up everything, like a broom. She could feel twigs and leaves trapped in the tangles that no amount of combing with her fingers would help. She brushed her clothes with her hands, knowing it was useless, and quickly gave up.

David watched her climb the staircase and said, "Shall I try to guess where you've been?"

"No, forget that. You'll soon know. First, tell me, where did Doctor Montalvo come from?"

"What do you mean, where did he come from?"

"I mean, where was he born, where was he living when..."

"I've no idea. My mother met him on the plane returning from Acapulco. The same time we visited Playa Blanca. Ten years ago. You know, when I first met you."

His answer troubled her. She had wanted something concrete to build on. There was one thing. "Doctor Montalvo did not live in Playa Blanca," she said firmly. "I knew everyone there."

David said, "He wasn't on the plane from Playa Blanca. I said Acapulco. But why is it important to know about him?"

"I wish I knew. I only know that there's a connection between him and my father. There's something going on in that locked room that has to do with why my father is gone."

He turned to look at her, his eyes alert with interest. "What?"

"It has to do with Villa Rey."

An eyebrow lifted.

"David, what do you know about Villa Rey?"

"Nothing. I don't even know where it is. What do you know?"

"Only that Señor Otero, Jim Donald and Doctor Montalvo all mentioned it today." She told him about her conversation with Juan Otero and then what she had seen and heard from the locked room. And as she talked, David's mood showed on his face.

First, it was an eager interest, then disbelief, and finally, anger.

"It all adds up," he said. "I knew my stepfather was into something crooked. Something that's using up my mother's money. Keeping a crew at an archeological dig would do that." He pressed his mouth into a thin, tight line.

"Why do you think that?" Elena said. "Is there something you haven't told me?"

"Yes," he said with a sudden grin. "I haven't told you about the mud on your chin and your nose. And that's all. Look, Elena, everything will work out. I'm not sure how, but it will. Try not to worry too much."

"All right. I'll try not to worry, but I'm not going to sit still. The first thing I'm going to do is read that letter and deed again. To see if Villa Rey was mentioned, or the hundred-year business."

"I'll bet the first thing you do is wash your face. Bring the papers out here, will you? I'd like to see them, too."

Thirty minutes later Elena moved restlessly on the top step of the outside staircase as she folded the documents and returned them to their envelope. There had been no reference to Villa Rey, but the instructions regarding what should happen in one hundred years was there. "That means it *is* the same land," she said. "Maybe it was called something else then." She sighed and her shoulders slumped. "I wish I knew what was happening. It's pretty confusing. Here and there a fact or two seems to make sense, but mostly, no. For instance, what am I doing here?"

"That's what I asked," David said.

"No you didn't. Not exactly. You asked how I fit in, and what I'm wondering is how do I happen to be here? It was Sylvia's letter that brought me, I know that, but Doctor Montalvo isn't Sylvia's friend—your mother is. But it's not your mother that's connected to whatever my father is doing—it's Doctor Montalvo.

"Unless you believe in fate," David said with a shrug, "you have to accept coincidence. But, hey, didn't you tell me that when you first talked to him, Montalvo was ready to send you packing and then changed his mind?"

"Yes."

"What made him change his mind?"

"I don't know. He was very brusque and businesslike until, like a clumsy fool, I kicked my purse across the floor, spilling most of my stuff out of it. He helped me pick my things up, handed them to me, and was suddenly very kind. He told me to sit down and brought me a glass of sherry. Then he asked me my name. David! Of course! He saw this envelope. He saw the word Tamaulipas on it!"

"That's it. Right then he guessed who you were. When you gave him your name, he knew. So he kept you around until he could figure out how you might help him."

"But the letter from Sylvia Lewis?"

"If you'd been someone else with that letter, Montalvo would have given you money for a hotel. Even if mother objected, he would have persuaded her that was the best thing to do."

"I guess so. No wonder he was so generous about Carlos." Elena held her hands out, palms upturned. "Well, I certainly haven't given Doctor Montalvo what he was looking for. All I have is questions."

"Wait until your father returns. He'll have the answers."

"That's just what Juan Otero said. Wait. I guess that's all there is to do."

The staircase was narrow, and they were very close to each other. The warmth of his breath brushed her cheek lightly as he said, "I won't be around to wait with you. I have to leave right after dinner."

"Tonight? I thought maybe you'd be here until the fiesta. When will you be back?"

"Friday, I hope. Saturday, for sure." He stood up, pulled her up beside him, and kissed her. He held her close for a moment and then, pressing a couple of dry leaves into her hand, said, "You're going to have to do something about your hair. I swear there are spiders in it."

"I'll brush it."

"Well, go do it. I have to get something from the car for mother. Meet me here after dinner. Okay?"

She watched him cross the lawn, already feeling lonely. When he disappeared, she reached for the knob of the door that led from the balcony into the upstairs hall. She stopped when she saw that the door was moving. Someone inside was closing it with great care. Someone, she thought, who'd been eavesdropping. Angrily, she pushed it open. The door bumped heavily and a high, squeaky voice said, "*¡Dios mio!*"

Elena slid into the hallway through the half-open door and found Sara picking herself up from the floor. "Are you hurt?" she asked.

Sara rubbed her upper arm. "No," she said sullenly.

"In that case, will you please tell me what you were doing? Were you listening to David and me?"

"Ay, señorita, how can you say that?" Sara's eyes shifted nervously and her hands fumbled in the pockets of her full black skirt. "I was...I was looking for the boys. I have this candy for them." She pulled a little plastic bag from her apron pocket and pressed it into Elena's hand. "Carlos says he loves coconut candies, and I promised them to him."

"For a look at my letters?"

Sara shrugged. "Perhaps. But I was only trying to help. He is so lonely for his Papá. And what harm was done?"

"*What*? You ask a little boy to cheat and steal, and you invade my privacy and read my letters and you..."

"And who was harmed?" Sara said stubbornly.

"No one, I guess," Elena said with reluctance. She had been ready to say a thing or two regarding the rudeness of eavesdropping when her conscience prodded and asked what *she* had been doing at Doctor Montalvo's window. "All right, Sara. Let's forget it." She went down the corridor to her room.

At dinner that night, David and Ana talked easily while Doctor Montalvo ate in almost complete silence. He addressed a remark or two to Mario and one to Ana regarding the dressing on the salad, but that was all. At the end of the meal he said to Elena, "Come into my study after dinner, please. I should like a chance to speak with you."

Doctor Montalvo's remark caught Elena in the middle of a mouthful, and she swallowed slowly and carefully, afraid she might choke. This was it! He had found out about her spying. "Yes, of course, *señor*," she said when she could finally speak. "I will be there." She caught David's look and added, "I'll need to go upstairs for a moment first," and Doctor Montalvo nodded his assent.

Ana poured coffee and said, "David, you'll be sure to be back for the fiesta, won't you? Salvador has invited some important newspaper people from Mexico, and I want you to meet them. And remember, you promised to give us a hand with the piñata."

"I plan to be here," David said. "I promised Mario, too."

Immediately after dinner, Elena waited for David at the top of the outside staircase. When she saw him bounding up toward her, she said, "I watched you at dinner and I could almost read your mind working. You're going to be busy with more than school, aren't you?"

"Yes. There's some snooping I have to do while Montalvo's tied up with his students' finals and the fiesta. My mother ran into a receipt for a storeroom that he rented. She doesn't think it means anything, but I do. Especially now, with what you saw and heard."

She said, "Maybe he keeps the things from Villa Rey in that storeroom until he brings them here."

David put his hands on her shoulders. "Do me a favor, Elena. While I'm gone, stay out of the snooping business, will you?"

"And you," she said, her voice calm enough above unexpected fears, "you be careful, too."

They walked hand-in-hand into the house and down the stairs to the entry hall. She watched as the front door closed behind him, and all the disappointments of the last few days lumped together to make this one greater. But it was the hum of the Porsche's motor passing the house that brought her a sense of doom.

The entry hall, well lit by its ornate iron chandelier, suddenly seemed dark and ominous. She pushed open the sliding glass door that led to the terrace and stepped out. The air was still. Below her, sprinklers were watering the sloping lawn. The rich smell of damp earth made her homesick for summer evenings in Playa Blanca, summer evenings when water hoses ran in the bordered yards of all the small houses and there was laughter and talk on the steps and the porches. Impatiently, she brushed a tear away. Home. You're thinking of home because you're frightened, and this is not the time for that. She walked back into the house. At Doctor Montalvo's study door, she hesitated. Then, squaring her shoulders, she raised her hand and knocked.

Doctor Montalvo was standing by the corner fireplace. "Come and sit down, Elena."

She took the chair by his desk.

His face was serious and friendly as he pulled up an armchair close to her. "I have been meaning to have a visit with you," he said. "This seemed to be an appropriate time."

A visit. With her? She looked down at her hands and said nothing.

Doctor Montalvo said, "I have been wondering... Sylvia Lewis...how was it that she came to write that letter to us?"

Elena sat up, surprised. "I suppose she was concerned about me. She still imagines me a child."

"Did Mrs. Lewis think we would be able to help you find your father?"

"No. Why should she? We all expected him to be in his house on Emerald Avenue."

"I see," he said mildly. "So you have had to conduct your own search." He leaned back in his chair and looked at her through half-closed eyes. "What did the girl have to say?" he asked abruptly.

"Girl? Oh, Luisa. Nothing... I mean, I decided not to give her the money. I am so sorry. I should have returned it to you before."

A glance from him, sharp, penetrating. "So you do not need her information."

Elena's neck was tense, her mouth dry. Her hands, which had been open on her lap, were now tight fists. She was being prodded to tell him something. "I don't need Luisa at all anymore," she said, controlling the anger that was threatening to break through.

"Ah-h," he said, "then you do know how to find him."

"I wish I did. The sad truth, señor, is that I am no closer to finding my father today than when I came here."

A look of something like anger flicked across his face. "So? Does that mean that you are giving up the search?"

She would never give up, but she was not going to let him know that. "I might as well," she said. "I have nothing to go on."

"Strange, I understood that..." His words ended as a frown began.

She smiled a tight little smile and stood up. "Señor," she said, "if you will excuse me, I should go upstairs and help the boys now."

If he replied, she did not hear him because there was a loud knocking on the study door. Doctor Montalvo stood up as the paneled door flew open.

"Professor," Jim Donald said, "look at this." He was holding a length of torn and muddy paper toweling and the tools she had hidden under the shrubs.

For a moment Elena's mouth hung open. Then she took a deep breath and forced a smile on her face as she slid by Jim into the hall. Going up the stairs, her feet seemed as heavy as her thoughts. If they find out that I was the one, and they might, Doctor Montalvo will know that I overheard them. Or that I saw something. He may decide that I am closer to finding my father than I said—than I really am. And what will he do then?

CHAPTER TWENTY

For the next two days, Elena kept waiting for "the other shoe to drop," but Doctor Montalvo said nothing to her about the towel-wrapped tools Jim had found. The thought of them, however, was never far from her mind, even though the days were full and surprisingly busy.

There was the piñata to finish, and it was more of a task than she had expected. Their lamb had white curls and a pink nose, yes, but it also had elongated ears and squatty legs that would require a lot of fixing. Mario said it looked a lot like a rabbit and why didn't they leave it alone and call it a "lam-bit." Elena, between disappointment and laughter, said they would work on it a bit more before making that decision. There was also her driving test to be taken, and, although the instructor assured her that she was ready, Elena had doubts that left her cold and clammy. But on Wednesday afternoon—by the grace of a good memory, a good instructor, and a good supply of saints to call on—she passed both her written and road tests. Finally, she was standing before the Department of Motor Vehicles' camera, trying to erase a grin of happy relief from her face before the camera caught it. She didn't make it. She was still smiling when she was handed a temporary license and assured that her permanent one would arrive within weeks.

When she returned to Gray Ridge Drive, Ana held out a pair of car keys. "These are for you," she said. "If you need the car for something personal, it's all right to use it. Just let me know."

On Thursday afternoon Elena had her first driving assignment. She was to take Ana to keep an appointment with her eye doctor. The white Cadillac would be in her charge, and so would Ana's safety. She was glad for the responsibility. She had had feelings of guilt at accepting so much kindness from Ana and giving so little in return. Compared to dealing with patients and cleaning up examination rooms for Doctor Flores, working for Ana was pure pleasure. Besides, she was ready for the challenge of a drive into the city. So why, she asked herself, are my hands clammy?

Once they were in the car and on their way, however, she felt more at ease. Ana chatted idly, apparently comfortable. Elena angled a glance at her. Yes, Ana was relaxed. Well, and why shouldn't she be? she thought. I can handle things, can't I? A few minutes later, at the entrance to the parking garage of the medical building, Elena answered herself. There were some things she couldn't handle. Facing a wooden barrier, she had waited for someone to come and lift it, finally pressing the horn for service. That was when Ana patted her shoulder. "It's done electronically. You have to push that red button, dear."

What made it even worse, Ana had to point out the ticket that needed to be removed for the barrier to rise.

Except for some stop-and-go traffic, the drive home was easy and uneventful. Even so, Elena found that she was extremely tired. When Ana suggested a stop at The China Cup, she nodded eagerly, glad to get out of the car.

They sipped their tea silently until Ana said, "What the doctor told me was more or less favorable. My eyes, it seems, aren't getting any worse. So long as I use my medication, he says, they'll be all right."

"That's good news, isn't it?"

"I guess so...except that he doesn't understand why I'm not able to read sometimes, or sew, or even watch television. All his tests suggest that I should be able to do whatever I want, including daytime driving." Ana paused, a vague uneasy look covering her face. "It's hard to believe, but he says that acute distress could make my vision fluctuate this way. Of course, he asked me a lot of questions..." Her voice trailed off and she stared out the tea-room window.

Elena wanted to comfort her and she searched for a way to do it. "The piñata is almost done," she said. "You should see it. Mario thinks it looks half-lamb, half-rabbit." When she got no response, she went on. "The fiesta, Ana. Are things going well with the plans?"

"All right, I think. Usually Salvador is more in charge. This year he has other things on his mind."

Yes, thought Elena, he does. He and I have the same worry. How to find my father.

But that worry, or any other, seemed not to burden Doctor Montalvo that evening. At dinner he was surprisingly jovial, discussing the fiesta with Ana, congratulating Mario and Carlos on their progress in speaking Spanish and English.

Elena looked around the table. A bouquet of spring flowers was in the center. The glassware and china gleamed in the soft light. Mrs. Addison's cooking, as always, was delicious. Carlos, for a happy change, was on good behavior. Everything seemed just right. Except Doctor Montalvo. He was overflowing with friendliness, when last night he had been, if not unfriendly, quiet, his eyes clouded with concern. Something had happened to make him happy. That troubled Elena.

Right after breakfast on Friday, a thin, glum-faced man and a little round woman knocked at the kitchen door. Elena, in the kitchen to find Carlos, looked on with interest as Mrs. Addison herded them to the table, sat down with them, and proceeded to give them a long list of instructions. The extra help for the Fiesta de Mayo had arrived, and with them came a heavy spring rain.

The rain will ruin everything, Elena told herself, thinking of the fiesta. And then she realized that she had a more immediate concern. Carlos. He would be soaked before the day was through. She sent him upstairs for his sweater and waited for him at the front door. When Carlos returned, he was wearing rain boots and a yellow slicker.

"They're Mario's. His mother said I should wear them." And then, in a whisper, he added, "They're silly. Do I have to wear them?"

Elena had time only to whisper "Yes" before Mario came up to them.

"See, Elena?" he said. "Now we'll really fool everybody. They're gonna think Carlos is me."

"Until he turns around," Elena said.

"Maybe not even then," Mario answered seriously. "The kids at school think we look alike."

"Maybe you do," Elena said. "Go on, here comes the bus."

The rain kept falling during the rest of the day. And on and off during the rest of the day, Mrs. Addison looked out of the windows into the sky and clucked anxiously. By late afternoon she was heaving great sighs, her generous bosom rising and falling in slow motion.

"If this goes on much longer," she told Elena, "the fiesta will have to be brought indoors. And Mr. Addison and myself, along with the new help, to be sure, will be up all night moving furniture around in the sitting rooms."

"Is there anything I can do to help, Mrs. Addison?"

"No, my dear, nothing anyone can do. Another few hours will tell the story. It's the waiting that's the burden, don't you know."

But the storm, to everyone's satisfaction, was gone before supper. After finishing the meal, Elena trailed the boys up the stairs and paused at her favorite spot, the window at the top. The moon, brilliant as a newly stamped coin, was sliding out from behind surging gray clouds. The trees at the edge of the woods and the shrubs on the grounds were spangled with moonlit drops of water. She caught her breath. Beautiful! Tomorrow night's glowing lanterns and garlands of colored lights would never decorate the garden like this.

On the lawn near the back of the house she saw the shrubs move, losing their jewelled drops of water. They moved again, parting, and two men slipped through them. The men rounded the back corner of the house, hugging the shadowed wall, and vanished behind the gate of Doctor Montalvo's patio. Almost immediately, a flickering light appeared in the study.

Now, below her in the entry hall, she heard muffled footsteps and the quick opening and closing of a door. She leaned over the railing and craned her neck toward the back of the house. There were no lights in Doctor Montalvo's study. Whatever was going on in there was going on in the dark. It was clear that he didn't want anyone to know about his visitors. For some unexplainable reason, that terrified her. Her hands were cold and wet as she ran up the stairs and down the corridor. Instead of going to her room, she raced to the telephone. Quickly, she dialed La Fonda, but before the connection was completed, she put the receiver back on its cradle. What would she say to Señor Otero? That she was frightened? That there were strange things happening that she didn't understand? And, if she did, what could he do to help her? Nothing.

Back in her room she walked straight to the balcony doors without lighting the lamps. She opened both doors wide, breathing deeply of the clean, moist air. The moonlit garden was still, peaceful. No threat lurked there. If there was a threat, it was inside, in Doctor Montalvo's study. Something was going on there that made her afraid. And underneath that fear was something else. She was tired, let down. Too much had happened in a little more than a week. The happy things—David, Ana, and the anticipation of tomorrow's fiesta—had shriveled into a back corner of her mind, leaving her with this odd, heavy feeling. She gripped the railing and looked up at the sky. And, as if asked, the moon slipped behind a cloud, leaving a pale darkness that suited her mood. She walked to the end of the balcony, dragging her gloom with her. But in a moment the moon reappeared, and with it her good sense.

She went inside, closed the doors, and lit the lamps. Whatever was in store for her in the years to come, she was sure of one thing: there would be other occasions with fear. It was time she learned to handle it. There was no use in running to a kind Juan Otero—or a protecting father, if she could find him—with flimsy fears, fears woven out of fantasy.

If they could, of course, they would give her comfort, but the trembling inside of her would remain. All right, so there *was* a little trembling there. She was a bit shaken, yes, but that didn't mean that she or the world were going to fall apart.

She turned back the blankets on the bed and walked down the hall to get Carlos. It was time to rest her body as well as her overworked imagination, time to wait for facts. But, as Santa Teresa was her witness, Mrs. Addison was right. The waiting was the burden.

CHAPTER TWENTY-ONE

Perhaps it was the cold clearness of the air that helped Elena to sleep soundly. The night, which she had expected to be wakeful and long, passed quickly. And perhaps it was the good night's sleep—or the thought that David would be back today—that made her feel more optimistic, even happy.

Breakfast that morning was much the same as other breakfasts, but the rest of the day was not. The house hummed with unusual activity. All hands were called in to make up for the hours the storm had stolen. Mr. Addison and the new man lost no time in constructing a platform by the pool.

Mrs. Addison nodded approvingly at the wooden structure. "For the men with the music, the mari...mari..." She struggled with the word.

"Mariachis," Elena said with a little laugh. "Mariachis, too! How wonderful!"

Sara, polishing a table nearby, looked up sharply, opened her mouth as if to speak, but instead walked quickly away.

Shortly after noon Jim Donald appeared, carrying folding chairs and tables from the playroom. When Elena dropped a basket of crepe-paper flowers on the grass, he sprinted over to help her. Although he said nothing, he pressed her hand for a moment and his usual cocky grin disappeared. As they stood up, a troubled look flashed across his face. "See you," he said. He strode away, only to stop and call over his shoulder. "Take care, huh?"

Why? Elena pushed the question away, but the dark look on Jim's face remained with her

An hour later she went to the kitchen for a glass of water. At the door she turned back. The kitchen was crowded with people—Mrs. Addison and Sara and a half dozen caterer's assistants—along with a mountain of well-wrapped trays and boxes of food. Elena got her drink in the pool house. On the way out she found Sara waiting by the door.

"Hello," Elena said. "Are you looking for me?"

"Yes," Sara answered. Then she bit her lip and shook her head. "No," she said, "no. I made a mistake. I am sorry." She whirled around and scurried toward the kitchen.

Elena stared after her and shrugged. There must be something in the air, she thought, that's contagious and that makes people act peculiarly.

It was twilight when Elena arranged the last paper flower on the musician's platform. She turned with a sigh of satisfaction to discover Sara looking at her from the kitchen door. Sara's lids dropped over her eyes, and Elena saw that her hands were playing nervously with the edge of her apron. What a strange little woman. I wonder what she wants.

"Sara," she called, "do you want to talk with me?"

Sara's head turned in a jerky circle, scanning the garden. Finally she nodded and slid out the door, beckoning for Elena to follow. They went around the east wing of the house and then behind the garages to a corner darkened by tall shrubs. There Sara stopped and turned.

"I have to say something to you," she said in a low, hurried voice.

Elena wanted to answer something flippant, something like, well, what a surprise, but a serious note in Sara's voice stopped her. "Yes," she said, "what is it?"

"This. This place is not good for you. If I were you I would..." Her voice faltered and stopped.

"What?" Elena said, wondering where this was leading. "What are you talking about?"

"Carlos and you. You should leave right now. With the fiesta going on, who will miss you, eh?"

"But, Sara, why should I?"

"Because you do not belong here," Sara said in a choked little whisper. "Take Carlos now...and go!"

Elena stared at her open-mouthed. Finally she said, "I won't do that! What is this? Why are you telling me this?"

"Because of Carlos. I like him. He is a good boy." Sara took a few steps to the corner of the garage and looked toward the house. When she returned, she said, "Listen, I do not have time to explain things. Trust me. It will be best for everyone if you take Carlos and go now."

"Now?" Elena stared at Sara. This was the woman who had bribed her brother into taking her letters, who had been caught eavesdropping on

David's and her conversation, who was probably a troublemaker and a liar. Trust her? Why was she even listening to her? "I don't believe you," she said. "I don't believe one word. Before I could, I would have to ask the Montalvos if..."

"No! No! Don't tell them what I have said!" Sara put her hands on either side of her face and groaned. "Doctor Montalvo will know that I heard."

"Heard what?"

Even in the shadowed twilight, Elena could see that Sara's face was pinched and white. "Nothing," Sara said hoarsely, "nothing. I should not have talked to you."

"Maybe not. But you did. So tell me. What's all this about my leaving?"

Tiny beads of moisture had collected above Sara's lip. She wiped them away with her apron. "Nothing. I must go now. They will be looking for me."

Elena watched Sara disappear around the corner of the garage and then crossed the lawn to the outside staircase. Strange. The whole thing with Sara is strange. Why does she want me to leave? And why right now? She shrugged. Who knows? Maybe not even Sara. That poor woman is so upset about something that I don't think she knows what she's talking about.

Once in her room, Elena pushed thoughts of Sara out of her mind. Draped on the bed was the embroidered red skirt Ana had lent her. She scooped it up and twirled around the room. How long had it been since she had been to a party? Over a year. And a party in a place like this? Never! In less than an hour, there would be music and dancing, and David would be back. She paused in front of the mirror, held the embroidered skirt up to her face, and smiled.

With bathing and dressing, the hour managed to pass and at last it was time to go downstairs. Carlos, waiting by the hall door, whistled. "What do you know, Elena? You look pretty."

"Thank you," she said. "I guess that means we're ready." She picked up a fringed red shawl. "Let's go." Carlos and Mario raced ahead of her down the outside staircase and were lost in the mass of people shifting about in the garden and terraces.

The fiesta was well under way. Elena paused on the staircase, searching the crowd for David. If he was down there, he was well hidden. There were people of all ages, including the children, whose pastime, it seemed, was to scurry in and out of the crowd. There were strolling guitarists, too, and, getting ready on the platform, a mariachi band. The air was bubbling with bits of laughter and chatter and the popping of corks.

Leaning on the railing, she watched eagerly as the guitarists wandered from group to group, strumming and singing. In a few minutes they disappeared and the people drifted to long white-covered tables gleaming with silver and crowded with deep dishes and platters of steaming Mexican food.

She hurried down the rest of the stairs and went to the corner she had discovered the night of the barbecue, the corner beyond the swimming pool and the musicians' platform. She sat on the wooden love seat behind the small lemon trees and the azaleas, and from her quiet shelter continued to watch the people.

Doctor Montalvo was not where she could see him, but Ana, looking beautiful in a sea-green chiffon dress, was near the stairs to the main terrace, talking to two attentive young men. In a moment she smiled and nodded and moved away from them, stopping at this table and that. The musicians on the platform announced their readiness with a blare of music, and the cleared area on the far side of the pool filled with dancers. Through an opening in the mass of turning and twisting bodies, she saw Ana talking to a man in white pants and a yellow shirt. She jumped up. David! In front of her the pink azalea dropped a shower of loose petals. She lowered her gaze to the spread of pink at her feet and when she looked up she saw that she was wrong. The man in yellow was not David. She sat down again. During the next few minutes, she scanned the crowd carefully, still looking for David, still unable to find him.

She was not the only one keeping an eye out for David. Mario and Carlos and two other boys appeared from nowhere and formed a semi-circle in front of her.

"Where's David, Elena?" Mario asked. "Mother says he's gonna help with the piñata."

"I wish I knew where he was. Still, he said he would be here, no?" Mario nodded. "Well, then, he will." She stood up. "Look over there. Your mother's found someone to pull the rope of the piñata. You four are going to miss your chance if you stay here. Someone else will break it and you'll miss out on the candy and the..."

Before she had finished, the boys were racing toward the garages where a type of scaffolding had been set up. From it dangled the papier-machê lamb, white curls moving softly in a light breeze. Perhaps the legs *were* too short, but from this distance... Under the piñata stood Ana, Mr. Addison and the man in the yellow shirt surrounded by a group of children. In a few minutes she saw Ana pick her way carefully toward the main party.

When she neared her, Elena called, "Do you need help with the children?"

"There you are, Elena. Is David with you?"

"No, I haven't seen him. Is he back?"

"If he's not with you, he's not back. I don't know where he is. All I know is that he's trying to prove something to me, and he's spending a lot of time doing it." She looked around her in a quick, anxious way, her eyes darting back to Elena. "He should be here, not chasing after proof for his bizarre ideas." Ana looked away again. When she finally turned back and spoke, her voice was calmer. "I'm sorry, I shouldn't be troubling you with that. It's between David and me."

I know David's ideas, Elena thought, and they are not so strange. Oh, Ana, if only I could tell you.

Ana said, "Why are you hiding in this corner? Come with me. I'll introduce you to a nice young man."

Later, much later, she tried to remember the nice young man's name, but all she could recall was that his laughter was contagious and that his dancing was effortless and fun. Once Ana had introduced her to him, he did not leave her side. He insisted that she take one sip, just one, of his champagne, and then whisked her off to the dance floor. Two or three other fellows asked to meet her, and he refused to give her up to them. And, although David never quite left her mind, Elena knew that she was having a wonderful time. One hour and a half later she was as reluctant to leave the party as her laughing companion said he was to lose her, but it was bedtime for the boys, and she had been instructed earlier that Mario was her charge.

"But I'm not sleepy," Mario whined when she had rounded them up. "It's only ten-thirty."

"Eleven," she said. "And I was told to take you up long before this."

"So?" Carlos said in his new English. "Make us a break, okay?"

"No," she said above Mario's laughter, "no."

The boys grumbled and complained, but half an hour later they were in their beds. She waited until

Carlos seemed to be asleep, picked up his clothes from the floor, and returned to her room. She had enjoyed the party, but now with the worry of David she knew there was no use in returning. She would wait on the balcony. As she stepped through the French doors, she heard a low whistle. The sound was close at hand, and she looked over the railing to the ground below her. There was no one there. The whistle again. She turned. David was sitting on the floor in a shadowed corner at the far end of the balcony.

"You look like something out of a painting," he said. "If I'd known what I was missing, I wouldn't have stayed away."

She sank to the floor beside him. "I am glad you're back. Your mother will be, too. She's been worried about you."

"Sorry about that. Sorry about being so late. I've been around for a while though. Down in a corner of the workroom as a matter of fact, talking with Jim Donald."

"With Jim?"

"Yes. I had to talk to him, to convince him that what Montalvo's been doing is more than just dirty, like misusing my mother's money, that it's damned illegal, like stealing from your father."

"But why Jim Donald?"

"Because we need him. I found that storeroom Montalvo's leased. I want him to show me what's in it."

For the first time, it seemed, real understanding hit her. David had been—was—waging a well-planned campaign to help his mother. He was coming at the problem from all sides, enlisting help where he could find it. "Will Jim do it?"

"He's weakening. But, in the end, it won't matter. Even though I don't get into that storeroom, some of the things people have seen going in there have convinced me absolutely. Now, if I can only convince Mother. She doesn't want to see what he's doing. She'll probably find excuses for all that I've discovered."

They were silent for a moment. The hubbub below them, the music, the voices, the laughter, all seemed far away. "You know, Elena," David said finally, "if your father presses charges, they could put Montalvo in jail for a long time."

"If my father ever returns," she said sadly. "And if he wanted to... press the charges, the way you said. If he did, it would hurt your mother, too."

David nodded. "Can't be helped," he said. He got up and pulled her to her feet. "I haven't really talked with Mother yet. It'll be a long session, but I'd better tell her some of what I've found out right now. The worst can wait." He squeezed her hand. "I'll look for you later."

"In the corner by the lemon trees?"

He nodded and she watched him go down the steps and disappear into the crowd. Then she started down the stairs. The scene below her was happy, carefree. But she no longer felt a part of it.

CHAPTER TWENTY-TWO

When Elena reached the bottom of the staircase, Doctor Montalvo was speaking from the platform. His gaze rested on her for a moment and then he smiled widely and gestured toward the musicians.

"The dance music will go on until two. At midnight, for the young and the vigorous, there will be a dance contest. And after the music stops, we'll share a Mexican tradition, *menudo*. For those whose taste is not yet attuned to our strength-giving broth, Mrs. Addison has prepared what she calls a modest hunt breakfast." He paused and laughed. "Modest. We shall see. We shall see."

When he finished, Elena was edging the crowd, moving toward the wooden seat where she had left her shawl. She had taken only a step or two in that direction when someone placed a hand on her shoulder.

"Elena, where you going? I've been waiting for you." It was the man she had danced with earlier, now taking her hand and pulling her toward the dance floor. "C'mon, c'mon, just one little dance."

"All right," she said not too reluctantly, "but just one."

They moved onto the dance floor. She stepped and twirled at a distance from him, then close to him, and then she was swept into a whirling turn.

The lanterns sped past in a glowing orange blur that included the musicians, then a group of smiling faces, and beside them, a somber one. Doctor Montalvo. He was watching her closely. As the music stopped, he turned on his heel and strode away.

She shivered and said something to her partner about the cold night air and about finding her shawl, and she left him. The bench was empty except for the fringed stole draped on the back of the seat. She pulled it around her, and her skirt rustled against the bench as she sat down. Now that David had returned, she was more at ease, and the waiting here was pleasant. How long she sat there, she didn't know, but the party was at its liveliest—voices and laughter and even the music were louder—when she heard the sound of running footsteps and a sharp whisper. "Elena!"

Carlos, in jockey shorts and a shrunken tee-shirt, ran from behind the oleanders.

"Carlos! What is going on?"

He was in front of her now, standing very still, his arms slack at his sides. Tears streamed down his cheeks as he said, "Mario's gone!"

"Gone? To his secret place? Oh, no, not again!"

"No, Elena!" His voice was shrill. "Not there! They took him! He kept yelling, 'leave me alone, leave me alone,' but they took him anyway!"

She put her hands on his shoulders. "What? Calm down. What happened?"

"I told you already. Two men wearing masks, like people in the snow, they came into your room and..."

"*My* room? Carlos, are you making this up? Is this a joke?"

"No! No! I tell you they came..." Carlos' voice broke and his words changed into gulping sobs as he sank heavily to the grass.

She looked at the twisted little bundle at her feet and bit her lip. Carlos rarely cried. Why was she doubting him? She slid off the bench to the grass beside him and put her arms around him. "All right, Carlos, I believe you. I am truly sorry. Now, can you tell me what happened?"

He nodded, still gulping. "We...we were in your room...playing hide and seek. I was hiding under your bed and Mario was...he was by my door counting."

"Yes. Go on."

"I heard some noises from the window and then I saw some big feet going toward the bathroom. I... I was scared, Elena. Pretty soon they came back and they had Mario. They were taking him out the window by the big chair and he was yelling all the time." Carlos pushed away from her. His eyes looked enormous in the shadowed light. "Elena, do something," he whispered.

She pulled the shawl from her shoulders and put it around him. "Wait here for me. I'll get Ana."

"No! Don't leave me!"

"All right. You can come with me." Under ordinary circumstances, Carlos would not have allowed a girl's shawl near him, but tonight he pulled it close to him. He was shivering. She put her arm around him. "Come on then."

Carlos followed her closely as she skirted the edges of the garden. Ana was nowhere to be seen. Finally she remembered. Ana was with David. As Elena wondered whether or not to look for her upstairs, she saw Doctor Montalvo. He was crossing the grass at an angle, smiling and nodding to his guests. He strode without a pause until he reached the gate to his private patio. She stiffened, thinking of the men she had seen the night before. This is no time to start scaring yourself again, she told herself. Mario is in trouble and his father has to know.

"Come this way, Carlos," she said, and rushed up the terrace steps. She went through the open glass doors into the entry hall, ignoring the eyebrows that raised at the sight of Carlos, red fringes of the shawl dragging, racing barefoot behind her. She pointed to the bench on which they had waited that first day. "Stay there," she said, and knocked on Doctor Montalvo's door.

"Yes. Who is there?" The words came loud and sharp.

"It is Elena, señor. I must see you!"

She heard quick footsteps and the door opened. Salvador Montalvo, his black eyes brilliant, his face flushed, said, "I have only a moment. I am expecting an important call." Then he reached out to touch her arm. "But you are agitated, señorita. You look as if you've seen a ghost. What is it?"

"Something terrible's happened!"

"Yes? Well, quickly, out with it."

"Kidnappers, señor!" she cried. "Two men. They broke into my room. The boys were playing hide and seek. Mario was in the bathroom counting. It was Carlos' time to hide. He was under my bed. And they took him, señor!"

Doctor Montalvo swung around and strode to his desk. "We must call the police immediately." He picked up the phone, but instead of dialing, asked, "Do you think this could be a prank? That he's merely hiding? Or run away?"

"Oh, no, they wouldn't do that. I mean make up such a frightening story." She felt anger spurt into her voice. "I can speak for Carlos. But as to running away, well, you would know about that better than I, señor. After all, he is your son, no?"

"My son?" He looked startled. "What do you mean?"

"That Mario didn't run away. I told you! Two men took him!"

Doctor Montalvo's face flushed scarlet and he said, "Not Carlos?"

"Carlos is just outside in the hall."

"Ah, I see. They took Mario." Something like anger crackled at the edges of his words.

She took a step toward the door. "I can call Carlos."

"No, leave him there. You may go now, Elena. I will take care of everything."

"But it was Carlos who saw everything. He can tell you..."

He brushed away the rest of her words with a move of his hand. "That will not be necessary."

"Shall I find Mrs. Montalvo for you?"

"That will not be necessary," he repeated in a dull, flat tone. "I want to tell her myself. You may go now."

In the hall she found Carlos right next to the door, the red silk bunched up around his neck. He was quiet as they went up the stairs. Once in their rooms, with the doors bolted behind them, he spoke.

"What will those men do to Mario? Will they hurt him?"

"Mostly they want money. They'll let him go if they get enough money."

"Does his father have enough?"

She nodded and changed the subject. "I think you had better get dressed. In case the policemen want to talk with you." Her gaze circled the room. Except for a small chair lying on its side, there was no sign of a struggle. But it had been an uneven match. Two grown men and Mario. David would want to know, but she couldn't look for him now; Carlos was too frightened to be left alone. She pulled the pillows out from beneath the bedspread and folded it back. "You can lie down on my bed until they call us."

Carlos shook his head and sat on the edge of the wing-backed chair. "Would they have taken me, Elena, if I had been the one counting?"

"You, Carlos? Who would want you, eh?" She glanced at him, a pillow pressed between her hands. "But it is strange. For a moment Doctor Montalvo thought it was you who was taken." She stared vacantly at the opposite wall. What had Sara said earlier? *It is important that you take Carlos and go—now.* And then something had frightened her.

Elena dropped the pillow and knelt by Carlos' chair. "Did the men say anything to Mario?"

He lifted huge, dark eyes to her face. "Yes, and it was funny. They said, 'Stop kicking, Carlos, stop kicking!'"

"Are you sure?"

"Yes, I am sure! Do I not have ears, Elena?"

She took his hand and squeezed it. "Yes, yes, you do. Now, don't worry about Mario. He'll be all right. Doctor Montalvo will get him back." She stood up and pulled him out of the chair. "Go get dressed as fast as you possibly can!"

"Why?"

She had no answer for him because she had no plan. All she knew was that she had to be ready. "Just dress please, Carlos." He nodded and then stole a strange little look up at her. Without another word, he went into his room.

While Carlos dressed she stood by the open French doors, trying to find an explanation for what had happened. It looked as though Doctor Montalvo had tried to kidnap Carlos. It made no sense. Why would he do that? Why? She knew now that even before she had met Doctor Montalvo he had been trying to find her father. But why the kidnapping? On that first day, after he had learned who she was, he had given her the job, even when Carlos made problems. The truth was that Doctor Montalvo had gone out of his way to persuade her to stay. He must have been sure that she would lead him to her father. And when he realized that she knew as little about where her father was as he did, maybe even less, he must have become desperate. "I have a plan to flush him into the open," he had told Jim Donald. But kidnapping Carlos? How would that be of any help?

Elena caught her breath and whirled around. Dear Teresa, why am I so blind? If her father heard that his son was in danger—and he would have because Doctor Montalvo had invited all those newspaper people from Mexico—he would drop everything to come to find him! And Doctor Montalvo could hold out for a ransom that included all that he needed in Villa Rey. She shook her head impatiently. No, no, she must be imagining it all. This was the kind of thing that happened only on television. Still, there was the secret room with all the secret happenings. She had seen that. And, tonight, there was Carlos running about in his underwear, frightened into tears, and there was Mario's disappearance, and the strange way Doctor Montalvo had acted when he learned that Mario was the one taken. *¡Basta!* Enough! Stop doubting yourself, Elena! It is absolutely clear what Doctor Montalvo had planned. Well, his plan has failed—at least, for now. Still, he's very determined to get what he wants. Which means? *He will try again, of course!*

She was back by her bed, tearing off the red satin skirt, the petticoats, the peasant blouse, and pulling on pants and a sweater. There was only one thing to do. Get away from Doctor Montalvo's reach as soon as possible. David would help her. He was here in the house with Ana. But where? Where? No, there was no time to look for him. Hurriedly, she stuffed the papers from under the clock into her purse and called Carlos.

His big eyes watched her as, with a signal to him to be silent, she stepped lightly to the balcony. She had to know where Doctor Montalvo was. She had to be sure he was busy, that he was somewhere where he would not see them before they went through the house to the outside. Below her the guests were crowded around the cleared area, watching the dance contest. She waited, and when the music stopped and the contestants had left the floor, Doctor Montalvo stepped up to the microphone. She slid back into the room and cautiously closed the French doors.

"We will go down the back stairs to the breakfast room," she said. "Whatever happens, let me take care of it. Try not to be frightened."

"I do not get frightened," Carlos said.

"Not too much," she said, and a half-smile came and went on her lips. She eased the door open and listened. "All right, Carlos," she whispered, "come with me. Be very quiet."

Moving quickly, they went down the hall to the gallery above the main stairs. Two young women with bright fresh lipstick came chattering toward them from the east wing, and Elena smiled and nodded and watched them go down the main staircase into the entry hall. The music had started up again. She grasped Carlos' hand firmly and ran across the empty corridor to the back stairs. The breakfast room was directly opposite the bottom of the stairs, and it had French doors that led to the side yard. Those doors, and the escape they promised, was what she was heading toward. Downstairs, she found the little corridor empty and the breakfast room brightly lit. She motioned Carlos to remain by the staircase and looked into the room. The table had been stretched to its greatest length and was covered with bowls and platters of cold foods. There were no people about. She reached across the corridor for Carlos' hand, ready to make a run for it, but then pushed him back. Sara, followed by two of the caterer's helpers, had rushed through the kitchen door to the table. Carlos whispered, "It's Sara," and started to speak, but Elena put a finger to his lips.

They stood silently in the narrow hallway, listening to the sharp ringing of silver on china, the muttered questions and answers, the quick footsteps and, at last, the sound of emptiness in the breakfast room. Cautiously, she looked around the side of the door. “They are gone,” she whispered. She put her hand firmly on Carlos’ shoulder and swept him to the other end of the room. There she fumbled with the knob, hoping the door would swing open quietly. It did. Carlos and she slipped out into the cool night air.

CHAPTER TWENTY-THREE

Elena's goal now was to get to the garage. Ten yards away was a shrub that shielded the workroom door from the swimming pool area. If they could make that undetected, they would be all right. "Come on, Carlos," she whispered, "run!" They raced across the brick walkway to the shelter of the shrub and, quickly, through the workroom door. Inside, she pressed her back against the wall, waiting for her eyes to get used to the dark, taking time to thank heaven and its inhabitants for getting her this far.

"Why are we hiding, Elena?"

Her hand tightened on her brother's. "No questions, Carlos. Just follow me."

They moved slowly across the darkness of the workroom floor to the entry to the garage. Beside her, Carlos moved like a ghost, only the sound of his quickened breathing giving him substance. In just half a minute—although it seemed more like ten—they had made it into the garage, and her eyes at last had adjusted to the dark. The outlines of the cars were clear now. The first one was David's Porsche. For an instant she thought she would write him a note, but she knew there was no time. Quickly, she moved past a station wagon and Doctor Montalvo's gray Mercedes to Ana's car. She gave

Carlos a little shove. "Get in. No, no questions. Not now."

He huddled in the front seat, saying nothing as she pulled the electronic garage door opener from the glove compartment. The great door lifted smoothly. She turned the key in the ignition and backed the Cadillac out on to the circular driveway. There were cars parked on each side of the curve, leaving only a narrow passageway, and she drove through it with painful slowness. But thank the saints for the loud music! Against it, the sound of the motor was like the ripple of a stream near a crashing waterfall. By the time she had maneuvered the car through the gates, her hands were wet with nervousness. She switched on the headlights as she drove through the little meadow, and before she swung on to the highway she slowed down and looked carefully into the rearview mirror. Only the mottled darkness of the woods was reflected there. No, they would not have missed her yet.

The headlights leaped out ahead of her, cutting the tall gray trees with a wide ribbon of light. She sighed and settled herself for the drive to the safety of La Fonda. Señor Otero had offered her help, and tonight she needed a place of refuge. Tomorrow? She could not plan ahead, but tomorrow, yes, she would call David. After that? After that would have to take care of itself. There was no time to think about it tonight. She glanced in the rearview mirror again and relaxed. No headlights showed behind her. For a while she drove silently, then she said, "You can talk now, Carlos."

When there was no answer, she shot a quick glance at him. Carlos was asleep, his chin resting on his chest. She wondered if he was dreaming. If he was, that meant that he was far away in a dream land and that she was here on this winding road all alone. Now she noticed how dark the trees were on each side of the asphalt, how the shadows thrown by the headlights danced away from her in unearthly patterns, and how there were no other cars on the highway. She sighed a shaky little sigh. There should be someone here to take care of *her*. Tears blurred her eyes. Angrily, she brushed them away. There was no time for tears.

Halfway down the hill, the car skidded through water as she took an unexpected curve. Carlos gave a little cry and sat up. "I'm sorry, Carlos," she said. "That was a bad turn."

With a little grunt of acknowledgment Carlos leaned against the headrest and was once more asleep. Driving now took all of her attention. The road went steeply downhill and the curves were short and sharp. However, once they were at the coast highway and stopped, she took time to scan the cars behind her. None looked familiar.

The clock on the dashboard showed two-fifteen as she brought the car to a rustling stop near the orange door of the restaurant. They were here at last and no one had followed them. She looked around. The boulevard was dark and almost empty.

In the middle of the block a street lamp smeared dim, yellow light on the sidewalk. Suddenly, as if from nowhere, a shabby bearded man stepped into the lighted area. Elena slid down in the seat and, shaking with sudden fear, hid her face in her hands.

A tapping at the window. She peered between her fingers at the bearded face pressed close to the glass. "Li'l lady," the man said, "d'ya have a quarter for a hungry man?"

Carlos looked up at the face beside him and with a sharp intake of breath twisted his body and buried his face in Elena's lap.

Elena pushed herself up. "Go away!" she shouted. "Go away! You're scaring my brother!"

"Aw, li'l lady, I wouldn' do that." Two grimy hands pressed on the window as the man straightened up. He tottered beside the car for a moment. "Wouldn' do that," he mumbled, and turned to walk back the way he had come.

"Sit up now, Carlos," Elena said. "He's gone." Carlos moved away from her, but kept his hand on her sleeve as they watched the drunken man amble down the block and disappear around the corner. She waited for another five minutes before she got out of the car. "We are safe now. Come on." Carlos followed her to the orange door.

The Oteros lived above the restaurant, she remembered that. But what she could not remember was whether or not there was a separate outside entrance. A pale night light showed above the curtains that covered the lower half of the cafe's windows. Stretching on the tips of her toes, she peered over them. There it was, a door in the wall behind the cash register. She would have to go through the restaurant to get to where the family lived.

The doorbell was to one side of the door. She pushed the button and a harsh ringing sound came through an open window on the second floor. She took a step back, stretching her neck to see if a light came on above them. When she looked down again, she saw a face at the restaurant window. Luisa was peering at her over the metal loops of the curtains. Luisa! And she had thought she was safe. She bit her lip, fighting back frustration. Everything was going wrong. From out of the shadows her aunt's voice rang wildly in her ears: "You're stringing beads without a knot at the end of the thread, María Elena! Use your head!"

Elena was pulling Carlos close to her, wondering what to do, when the lights came on inside the cafe. She saw Luisa swing around to face Juan Otero, who was standing in the doorway behind the cash register. He was wearing a plaid cotton robe and his hair was rumpled from sleep. His lips moved, and so did Luisa's—angrily. Whatever it was they said, Luisa rushed to the back of the restaurant and disappeared.

Elena whirled to the window and rapped on the glass. "Señor Otero!"

The orange door opened an inch, and then wider as Juan Otero said, "Señorita Elena! You! You knew. Somehow you knew to come to us."

She nodded, wanting to say something but not finding words.

It was Carlos who spoke. "We ran away, Señor Otero, we ran away!"

He looked down at Carlos. "And you came here. Yes, yes, this is a small miracle."

"Señor," Elena said, "may we come in?"

Juan Otero's brown face reddened. "To be impressed with miracles, " he said, "is one thing. To be rude, another. Come in, come in, and please excuse a rough old man." He herded them toward a booth.

Elena let Carlos slide into the booth and then sat down beside him. "We need your help, señor," she said wearily. "And the reason...well, that is a long story, not a miracle."

"Are you all right?" he asked.

"We are fine now that we are here. All we need is a place, just a little corner, to stay tonight." She shifted on the seat uncomfortably. Miserably, she said, "Luisa, *señor*...Luisa may not like it."

"Perhaps," he said. "But that is no concern of mine, or yours. Luisa is what you call 'out of grace.' Carmen and I will find you that little corner, and, whatever you are running from, you will be safe."

She gave a shaky little laugh. "Thank you. I don't want Doctor Montalvo to know where we are because he will know that...because he might..."

Her words stuttered to a stop. "Señor, I promise to tell you the whole story first thing tomorrow."

A soft creaking came from the swinging doors behind them as Elena finished, and both she and Juan Otero glanced in that direction. He shrugged, dismissing the sound, as he looked back at her. "Tomorrow will do," he said as he sat down opposite her. "I, too, have something to tell you. But my story cannot wait." Now Juan Otero's pleasant round face took on the smug look of a well-fed cat. A smile curved his mouth slowly as he said, "Your father, señorita. Your father is here. He came no more than an hour ago."

"My father?" she echoed. This was the news she had been waiting to hear for months, but for the moment its meaning evaded her. It was hiding somewhere behind a shade abruptly pulled down in her mind. She looked at him dumbly. "My father? Here?"

"Papá!" Carlos squealed. "Papá! Where? Where?"

"Upstairs, asleep on the living room couch."

Her father, here. The shade in her mind spun wildly, wound itself tightly and let in the light. "Carlos!" she said. "Did you hear?" She pulled her brother toward her and hugged him. "He's here, at last!" A sudden, somber thought made her turn to Juan Otero. "He is well? Not sick or hurt?"

"He is fine."

"But he...he...you didn't call me."

"Perhaps we should have called you." Juan Otero nodded briskly. "Yes, yes, that might have been better. But the hour was late, and to awaken a household. . .well, we decided to call you early in the morning. Of course, I had assured your father that you were in good hands. Forgive me if I did wrong."

"Wrong? No." His face blurred before her and tears spilled out of her eyes. "He is here, señor! Everything is right about that! Can we see him now?"

Señor Otero's face crinkled into a big smile. "To make certain that he is really there, eh? He is. Go up the stairs and to your left. Meanwhile, I will let my good wife know who rang the bell."

None of them had heard the opening of the door that led to the second floor. When a voice called, "Juan. *Amigo*, what is going on?" they turned, startled.

Elena didn't remember moving, but she was up and racing across the room into her father's arms. She pushed her face into his chest and forgot everything but the feel of his rough shirt on her cheek, the solid pressure of his strong arms and the sweet sound of his voice saying, "Elena, Elena, my girl. . . "

CHAPTER TWENTY-FOUR

Half an hour later, after hugging Carlos and assuring him that he would be there in the morning, Miguel Vargas carried his sleepy son up the stairs to the living room. Juan Otero and Elena followed.

Miguel lay Carlos on the couch, placed a cushion beneath his head and sat next to him. With great care, he adjusted the pillow against his leg, then brushed a few strands of hair away from Carlos' eyes.

Elena watched her father pensively. He seemed older. There was more silver showing in his hair and there were deeper furrows on his forehead. But there was more to it than that. The outline of his face seemed to sag, and his dark eyes, usually so direct and carefree, now had an uneasy look. Was she imagining it? No. He *was* different. But no matter. He was here, and the silver in his hair was handsome against the copper of his skin.

The glow of a floor lamp fell warmly on the brick-colored rug and rebounded to the couch. She pulled up a chair and sat down. "I can't believe you're here," she said.

Juan Otero grinned. "I have trouble with that, too."

Elena moved the chair closer to the couch. "Father," she said quietly, "couldn't you have written me? Just one quick letter?"

Miguel threw his head back and frowned. Then he scanned the room slowly, his eyes finally resting on her. "No, Elena, I could not write. If I had written to my family, the man might have traced me. That was a chance I could not take. He almost killed me once; he would have tried again."

"Who? Who would do that?" Even as she asked, an icy certainty stabbed Elena. "Why?"

"That's a long story. For now, it can wait." He smiled at her. "I want to know about you and your brother. Juan says you found work as a companion to an elderly lady. Is that right?"

"I found work, yes, but Ana is not old. And better than that, she is kind and generous—and even beautiful."

"Ah, well, so much the better. All that matters is that she has been good to you." He patted her knee. "And what does a companion do?"

Don't treat me like a little girl! she wanted to shout. She bit back the words, remembering that only an hour or so ago she had been longing for his protection. "We can talk about that later, too," she said. "Right now it's not important. What I need to ask is if you know a man named Salvador Montalvo."

"Montalvo!" her father said so sharply that Carlos groaned in his sleep. "Yes, I know Montalvo," he added in a dry, hard voice.

"Well, he is the man I am working for and..."

"*Working for Montalvo!* No! He's the man I'm talking about." Her father shot a look from Juan Otero to her and then back again. "And *you* working for him? How can that be?"

Elena thought back to how it had been, how Doctor Montalvo had woven a web for the two foolish flies that had wandered through his door, but she put that explanation aside. "What could I do?" she said. "When no one knew anything about you on Emerald Avenue, I needed help, and Sylvia Lewis... You remember Sylvia Lewis?" Her father nodded impatiently and she went on. "Sylvia had given me a letter to her friend, Ana Montalvo, and that's where I went. She had known Ana for a long time—long before she married Doctor Montalvo—when she was still Ana Martel."

"I see. No, your friend Sylvia would never put you near harm. How would she know who Montalvo was? To my knowledge he never set foot in Playa Blanca."

Elena said, "Sylvia Lewis met him later. She met him here, when she was visiting Ana, but I guess no one knew much about him even then. Including Ana. Even now, there are some things she doesn't know." She was silent for a moment and then added, low-voiced, "I think Salvador Montalvo is stealing from you."

"Stealing from me?" Her father's face puckered into a puzzled frown. "But what?"

"The treasures on your land."

He shook his head. "What are you talking about, Elena?"

Elena bit her lip. Everything is as mixed up as a snarled ball of yarn, she thought, and I'm not sure I can unravel it. She reached out and touched her father's hand. "Let me try to tell you. But let me start at the beginning, otherwise it gets all mixed up."

"Go ahead, go ahead. Tell it your way."

"First, I wrote you that I was coming to Los Angeles to live with you. And I came, even though you hadn't answered me. Mainly *because* you hadn't answered me." Elena spoke slowly, trying to remember clearly. She skimmed over her arrival at Emerald Avenue, and meeting the policemen, and going to Gray Ridge Drive, spending more time telling him how her suspicions had grown and what she had seen and heard. She tried to keep calm as she recounted the events of the last three days, but when she came to her talk with Doctor Montalvo about the kidnapping, her voice broke. "So, after that, I knew I had to get away from there. I took Ana's car. And here I am."

Across the room in a reclining chair, Juan Otero was leaning forward, listening intently. Her father, too, had become more and more alert as she talked. He had asked a few questions early in her story, but for the most part heard it silently, shaking his head at intervals. He had smiled when she told him about David, and his eyebrow rose. Now he said, "Sad, sad. And what is even sadder is that it was Montalvo who tried to kill me, and the man is my blood relative. He is my own first cousin."

Elena sat up. "Cousin? Of course! That's why he knew about your father's letter."

"Yes, he knew about it. My cousins on all sides knew about it. But none of them took it seriously. Or so I thought."

She said, "Thank God he doesn't know you are back. He'd be down here after you. I hope you were careful."

Her father said, "I was careful." And then, "That damned fool! As far as I am concerned, those Indian relics they dug up could have been his, or partly his..." He shook his head and smiled sheepishly. "Valuable, eh? Well, they fooled me. Of course I ran into the digging. I didn't say who I was, but I did ask questions. The two men working there convinced me they were just hauling building rock." He held his hands out, palms up. "Valuable, eh? Well, what does a carpenter know of such things? In any case, I am not sure now to whom those old pots belong. I have sold the land."

"You sold it?" Elena said. "To whom?"

Instead of answering, her father turned his head sharply towards the hall. She, too, had heard the shuffling sound. Juan sat up and looked over the back of the reclining chair. "Luisa," he called, "is that you?"

For a long moment there was silence and then Luisa's hushed voice said, "*Sí, Papá.*"

"Is there something you want?" Juan asked.

"No, Papá. But I...I couldn't help hearing. Those are terrible things that happened to Señor Vargas."

A streak of anger shot through Elena. That vicious little hypocrite! She's pulling strings—this time my father's. Standing in the doorway in a long cotton nightgown, Luisa appeared almost angelic. Her beautiful lashes fluttered as she said, "Good night," but the look in the narrowed eyes as they moved to Elena glittered with venom.

Elena moved uncomfortably, and her father stood up. "We are keeping your whole family awake, Juan. Look at the clock. It will soon be morning. This can all wait until later."

"No, no, Miguel," Juan protested. "Sit down. Elena cannot wait to hear your story—nor can I."

Her father glanced from Juan to her and shrugged in defeat. "*Bueno*," he said, settling back on the couch, "if you are not too tired. This is how it happened. Montalvo must have gotten word of that would-be surveyor I persuaded to go out to Villa Rey last fall. That is clear to me now. You see, last November Montalvo came to me and offered a substantial sum for what he called 'your worthless land.' He said, 'You're going to lose it anyway, unless you build something there by May fifteenth,' His offer was strange, of course. What could he hope to develop on the land in that short while?"

Elena said, "He wanted the Convent of the Little Sisters to get it by default! He had made some kind of arrangement with them. I heard him say that!"

"That was it, eh? Well, when he raised his offer, I became convinced that there was something of real value there, that maybe I should look into what I could do with it. And I had some ideas. That was when Montalvo decided to stop me." He took his eyes away from hers and looked at the floor. "So I kept my movements hidden. I was afraid to let him find me again. I...yes, I was afraid."

As Elena listened to her father, a soft feeling grew in the pit of her stomach. All the years he had lived, and he had been scared, too. She leaned forward and put her hand on his knee.

He covered her hand with his. "I am sorry for all I have put you through, my daughter. Juan explained what happened to my letters."

She said, "Señor Otero has been very good to me."

"And to me," her father said. "He loaned me the money to look into the possibilities." He turned to the other man, grinning. "What were they, Juan? A well? Yes, we were going to find water and dig a well, and then we were going to build a road to it. Ay, Juan, what lunatics we are! Still, we scared Montalvo." His face became serious. "I said I would repay you with interest, Juan, and I will. You see, before I had any answers as to whether water was likely and how much money it would take, I received surprising news. Something that Montalvo must not have known. There has been exploratory drilling going on in that area of the desert for years, but it was after Montalvo tried to buy it that oil was discovered on my parcel of land. Oil! Can you believe it?"

She heard Juan take in a quick breath. "Hombre, Miguel, you are a rich man now!"

Her father shook his head and said somberly, "Not rich, Juan. But a cup of clear soup is a feast to a hungry man. I had no trouble selling the land, of course. Still, I had to do it fast. May fifteenth was coming closer, and, as much as I respect the work of the good nuns, the land belonged to me and to my children, not to them. I couldn't wait." He glanced at her and then at Señor Otero, and there was a faint trace of a smile under his somber look. "My good father would approve of this kind of development on his square of desert. After all, it will help the Mexican economy. The government controls the oil in Mexico, remember? And as to the treasure he spoke of, those things belong in a museum. They should go to the government, too."

At some point during her father's story, Elena had come to the decision that she must make a call to David and Ana. That she should have made it earlier. That they would be worrying about her. She jumped up. "May I use your phone, Señor Otero?"

"Certainly. It's to your right at the top of the stairs."

Elena dialed the number and was surprised to find that the line was busy. Her first thought was that they were making calls about her; her second, that they were reporting the car as stolen. She waited impatiently and had started to dial the number again when the ringing of the doorbell ripped through the quiet.

Luisa, in jeans and tee-shirt now, flew past her. Elena caught a flash of the plaid robe as Juan Otero hurried after her. She dropped the phone on its cradle and followed Juan down the narrow stairs. She reached the doorway behind the counter in time to see Luisa throw the street door open.

"You!" Luisa said, taking a step back into the room.

"I'm looking for Elena," a familiar voice said. "Is she here?"

"David!" Elena cried. "Yes, I'm here."

Señor Otero turned back to look at her, then, with a frown, at Luisa. He said, "*Bueno, bueno*, come in, young man."

David stopped just inside the door. His black hair was untidy, hanging carelessly over his forehead, and he was wearing a grease-stained blue windbreaker that Elena recognized as one belonging to Henry Addison. He looked past the others to her. "Elena, what is it? Why did you run away?"

"Because I had to." Elena moved around the counter toward the door. "But everything is all right now. Señor Otero will let us stay here tonight."

"But why? What happened?" David looked suspiciously at Luisa, who had edged her way behind the counter. "And why here?" Juan Otero cleared his throat, and David turned to him. "I'm sorry, sir.

This is a helluva time to knock on your door, but I was pretty worried." He extended his hand. "I'm David Martel, and I need to talk to Elena alone."

Juan Otero nodded slowly as they shook hands. "Elena?" he said, looking at her, "do you wish to speak with this young man?" When she said yes, he said, "Luisa, come into the kitchen. You and I have something to discuss. We'll go up the back stairs."

When the swinging doors were still, Elena led the way to a nearby booth. She sat down. David started talking even before he slid in beside her.

"You've sure had me hopping," he said. "First, I went looking for you behind the swimming pool by the lemon trees—where we had planned to meet. When you didn't show, I went to your room and knocked. And when you didn't answer, I went in. Your dress was on the floor by the bed and a chair was turned over..." He raised his shoulders a bit. "Didn't take any more to tell me something was wrong."

"I know, I know. Let me tell you."

"Sure, tell me. Why the boys? When I found they were gone, I was really stumped. Why'd you take them? I mean Mario, too."

"Mario? Oh...oh, you don't understand."

"You bet I don't. None of it. For instance, why didn't you tell me you were leaving?"

"There was no time. You were talking with your mother."

He shot her a puzzled glance. "I searched that place from top to bottom, Elena. I was on my way to look in the woods when Mrs. Addison stopped me. Said she was sure she'd seen the Caddy leaving. I ran into the garage and sure enough it was gone. I knew where you were then. I told Mrs. Addison to tell Mother where I was heading, and down I came." He turned on the seat to face her. "Damned if I can figure what got into you. Why'd you run off? What made you think you could take Mario without telling anyone?"

It might have been the lateness of the hour, or the relief at knowing that her father was safe, or the sudden tiredness she was feeling—or the look of injured righteousness on David's face. Whatever caused it, Elena was unable to stop herself. She put her head down on the table and laughed. And once she started, she had a hard time stopping. Tears were streaming down her cheeks and onto the table when she felt David get up.

"Here," he said, putting a glass of water by her hand, "drink this." He remained standing as she lifted the glass and drank. "What did I say that was funny?"

"Nothing. I mean, yes, something. Please sit down, David. This will take a little while." She finished the rest of the water and started talking. But even with David's interruptions, the recounting of the night's events did not take long. "Poor little Mario," she said when she was through.

"Mario will be all right," he said. "Montalvo will see to that." His hand closed over hers on the table as he said, “I sure made a fool of myself. You oughtta punch me out.”

“I will. But another time. I’m too tired now.” She slid her hand from under his. “Will you let me out now?” As she pushed herself up from the booth, she heard the sound of hushed voices in the kitchen. “David,” she said, “while he is alone, come upstairs and meet my father.”

They walked toward the stairway, and as they did, the phone began to ring. The kitchen door swung open and Carmen Otero, dressed for the day and smiling, bustled into the room.

“*Buenos días, Elena,*” she said as she reached for the instrument by the cash register. “Your father is upstairs getting Carlos back to sleep. He is waiting for you.” She turned and spoke into the phone. And then, with her hand over the mouthpiece, she said, “Young man, are you David? This call is for you.”

David frowned and took the phone. Elena waited, hardly aware that Juan, also dressed and wearing his white apron, was in the restaurant now, that Luisa had followed him and was hovering near the kitchen doors. She was watching David’s face turn pale as he listened, and then hearing his urgent questions, “When? What was he…”

David nodded as the metallic sounds from the other end of the line continued, then said, “I see. I’ll be right there, Mrs. Addison. Yes, I’ll call the officers first.” He put the telephone down and turned slowly. “Elena, I can’t meet your father. Not now.

I've got to go. Montalvo...Montalvo... His car went out of control near Reinhardt Road. There was an accident. He's dead."

Elena took in her breath. She, too, had skidded on that wet pavement. "Dead? Are you sure?" And then, "Of course you're sure. Does your mother know?"

"Yes, she knows. The police have been there. They brought some of his things, including a paper that had Luisa's name and this address." He shook his head. "That really threw Mrs. Addison, because she knew I was here."

Juan whirled around to face his daughter. "What's this? What's this about your name?"

"I don't know," Luisa whined. "I don't even know what he's talking about."

Elena did not move. She stood still and let the pieces fall into place. Doctor Montalvo must have been coming after her—or her father. He had known where she was. And he had Luisa's name. That must mean... She swung around. "You called him!" she said to Luisa, and her words were shaky with anger. "The minute I got here, you ran to the telephone. What did you tell him? That I was here with the car? That my father was here? Did you tell him..." She stopped. Fighting with Luisa would help nothing. Leave her to Señor Otero. She looked down at her hands, a sob rising up from deep inside of her. So many terrible things had happened, and she seemed to be right in the center of them all.

David said, "May I use your phone, señora?"

While David made his call, Elena circled the counter and went up the stairs. At the top she paused and clung to the railing. "Father," she called. "Did you hear? Salvador Montalvo is dead."

Her father mumbled something and came to the doorway. "Dead?" he said. His eyes were puzzled, a little shocked. "Dead?"

"It was an automobile accident." No use to say that he had been on his way here. Later, there would be time for details. "It happened a couple of hours ago."

"While we were sitting here," her father said, shaking his head. "While you were downstairs, I was up here, struggling with myself, wondering how I was going to deal with Montalvo. And now there is no need."

Elena said, "I am struggling, too. I have to decide what to do. There's Ana."

"Ah-h, she will need you. That is it, no?"

"Yes." Elena looked up at him and grinned. "But she will also need her car. I have it, remember?"

"Ah, yes, the car." His hand pressed her arm. "And that young man?"

"Yes, I think he will need me, too." She cleared her throat. "But I just found you! And now I have to say goodbye."

He put a large comforting arm around her. "Do you want me to go with you?"

She rested her head against him and sighed. Then she raised it and said, "No, I'll go alone. It's Carlos who needs you. I will be all right."

Downstairs, she found David still talking. When he put down the phone, she took his hand and went out the door with him.

Outside, a faint glimmer of daylight showed behind the fading night sky. A pale white mist swirled above the rooftops, shrouding the lamppost in an amber veil. Moisture that had been collecting on the eaves fell drop by drop to the sidewalk below, and a cold little splash hit Elena's cheek. Like tears, she thought, like the tears I would not cry in there. "Was it my fault, David?" she asked.

"My God, no. No way, no possible way." He put his hands on her shoulders and smiled at her. "But I was thinking the same thing. Did I push him too hard? Did I force his hand? I don't think so. He was a self-serving person, willing to do anything to get his hands on those artifacts. When he got Luisa's call, he must've thought, there's still time; I can still stop Vargas from interfering. And he drove himself into an accident. No, sweet Elena, that's not our fault." He pulled her closer and they stood, arms around each other, thinking their separate thoughts. Then he kissed her. "I have to get out of here," he said.

"I know, I know. I'll follow you soon."

She watched David get into his car. Then she walked to the Cadillac and swung open the door on the driver's side. In the window above the restaurant she caught sight of two people looking down at her. Her father and a sleepy-faced Carlos. She nodded, waved goodbye, and sighed in sweet relief. Her father was back and Carlos was safe. But almost immediately that reassuring thought was shattered by a new one. Mario!

"Mario will be all right," David had said. "Montalvo will see to that."

And Montalvo was dead.

CHAPTER TWENTY-FIVE

By the time Elena left the coast road and started up the hill that led to Gray Ridge Drive, her mood had changed from near-terror to cold fear. She looked neither right nor left as she drove up the tree-bordered road, her eyes fixed on the ribbon of gray asphalt.

Then, when she reached Reinhardt Road, her gaze was drawn through the thin morning light to a broken wooden barricade and mangled shrubbery at the edge of the sharp curve. Her hands tightened on the wheel. This was where Doctor Montalvo had been killed. She shuddered and drove slowly until the highway became less twisting.

As she climbed, the trees grew more dense, some overhanging the narrow highway and shutting off the sky. She pressed down on the accelerator. She thought with dread of her arrival at the house on Gray Ridge, of the grief that at this moment must be engulfing Ana. It was not only that Ana's husband had been killed in a horrible accident, but that her son was still missing and in possible danger.

Elena was so sunk in her leaden thoughts that it was only a sixth sense that told her she had seen a movement at the edge of the road by The China Cup—and that someone had called her name. She slammed on the brakes and backed up slowly.

Half-hidden by shrubbery at the entrance to the restaurant was Mario. In rumpled, muddied pajamas, but it was unmistakably Mario. Thank the saints! How had he escaped the kidnappers?

By the time the car had reached him, Mario was jumping up and down wildly. "It's you! It's you!" he shouted. "I knew it was you!" He opened the car door and scrambled onto the seat.

Elena reached over and hugged him. "Are you all right?" she asked.

Mario nodded and pulled away. "David went right by me," he said, his eyes sparking with indignation. "Why didn't you come for me before, Elena? When they left me here, those men said you would."

"Left you here? Is this where you've been all the time?"

"Uh-uh. They drove around for a long time first. They kept talking to me in Spanish. They wouldn't believe I wasn't Carlos." Mario frowned and added, "But after a while maybe they did, 'cause they came here and used the telephone. And then we just sat in their dumb car."

"They didn't hurt you, did they?"

"Uh-uh. They just made me mad. I wasn't scared or anything, but I kept waiting for someone to come and..." A tear rolled out of the corner of his eye and he brushed it away angrily. "When they saw the police cars going up the road, they made me get out and told me to wait here until someone came for me. Then they drove away. It was dark... and nobody came...and after a long time I saw

David, but he went right by me." His voice had become a shrill little whisper and he was crying openly.

She patted his arm, found him a tissue, and said, "It's all right now, Mario." And even as she said the words, she knew it wasn't so. Mario had another sorrow waiting for him. "I'm taking you home."

When they reached the house on Gray Ridge, she swung the car across the gravel drive and stopped by the massive front door.

"Go on, Mario," she said. "Go straight to your mother. She's worried about you."

"Aren't you coming?"

"In a minute. Go on, go on. Straight to your mother."

Elena watched him race up the steps. Sara opened the door. Mario said a breathless hello and ran past her to the staircase. When the tall oak door closed, Elena sat staring at it, thinking of the day when she had first stood before it. On that day she had been looking for someone to help her, to take care of her. She hadn't yet found her father, so she had turned to Sylvia's friends, the Montalvos. She pictured the lovely room she had been led to and thought wearily of its big comfortable bed.

She shook her head impatiently. Stop wasting time, Elena! Put the car away. Wash your face. Comb your hair. There are people in that house who need you.